保定文化密码

讲述历史文化故事

②

Baoding Cultural Code

Telling Historical and Cultural Stories 2

保定文化密码

讲述历史文化故事 2

李会斌 主编

韩红梅
何远知 译

河北大学出版社

·保定·

出 版 人：朱文富
责任编辑：李　达
装帧设计：赵　谦
责任校对：李　易
责任印制：常　凯

图书在版编目（CIP）数据

保定文化密码 ： 讲述历史文化故事. 2 ： 汉文、英文 / 李会斌主编 ； 韩红梅， 何远知译. -- 保定 ： 河北大学出版社， 2023.2

ISBN 978-7-5666-2110-8

Ⅰ. ①保… Ⅱ. ①李… ②韩… ③何… Ⅲ. ①新闻报道－作品集－中国－当代－汉、英 Ⅳ. ① I253

中国国家版本馆 CIP 数据核字（2023）第 030880 号

BAODING WENHUA MIMA
JIANGSHU LISHI WENHUA GUSHI 2

出版发行：河北大学出版社
地址：河北省保定市七一东路2666号　邮编：071000
电话：0312-5073019　0312-5073029
网址：www.hbdxcbs.com
邮箱：hbdxcbs818@163.com
印　　刷：涿州市般润文化传播有限公司
幅面尺寸：145 mm×210 mm
字　　数：113 千字
印　　张：4.25
版　　次：2023年2月第1版
印　　次：2023年2月第1次印刷
书　　号：ISBN 978-7-5666-2110-8
定　　价：33.00 元

编委会

总策划　杨宝东

主　编　李会斌

副主编　席晓靖　单　娜

编　委　周　丹　吴超才　韩　朝

保定地域文化的时代书写

古城是保定人民心中的根与魂，地域文化是其最吸引人的所在。

两千余年的历史，在保定留下许多不灭的文化印记，成为独具特色的风土人情。在岁月洪流中，古韵流芳的亭台楼榭、传承沿袭的手工技艺、历久弥香的地方风味等历史文化遗产，被一代又一代保定人视若珍宝，精心呵护。它们不但没有随着时间而消失，反而完好地沉淀在古城的肌体里，成为熠熠生辉的一部分，生生不息。

了解一座城市的地域文化，最直接的方式之一是阅读这座城市的报纸。作为保定最具权威性与影响力的主流媒体，保定日报社当仁不让地肩负起这份增进文化认同、增强文化自信的责任与担当。

2019年正值中华人民共和国成立70周年，保定日报社精心组织策划了“壮丽70年·奋斗新时代——弘扬地域文化　讲述保定故事”大型系列宣传报道活动，百余篇报道在全媒体刊发推送，并集结为系列图书出版。我们用媒体人特有的方式，将藏在时间深处的故事唤醒，探索书写保定、宣传保定的新形式、新路径，从中感受到的历史光辉、文化魅力与时代脉搏，不仅是一种情感的寄托与共鸣，更是引领风尚、激励奋进的力量。

积淀深厚的保定地域文化，绝不是一本书可以言尽的。作为系列图书的第二册，本书在延续前作风格的基础上，讲述了淮军公所、古莲花池、天水桥等保定地域文化符号的“前世今生”。在悠久岁月中，它们见证了古城的沧桑巨变，是诗与远方的化身。当下，现代化品质生活之城建设如火如荼，属于新保定的新故事正在继续，它们也将在人们的保护下与自身的复兴中，更加完美地衬托城市的品质生活。

本着弘扬优秀传统文化的初心与使命，我们在记录城市的过去、现在和未来的过程中观察、思考，用新闻文化散文的笔触，源源不绝地讲述保定故事，传递保定声音。我们希望将这种浓浓的人文情怀传递给更多人，无论是远方游子，还是到访宾客，抑或是无意间读到了这些文字的人，都能从中感受到保定文化的厚重底蕴。

城市更新，古城不老。有生命的文化，一脉相承，在保定这块文化沃土上得到的滋养，令它们不断生长，鲜活而跃动。其中注入的时代所赋予的“新”，迸发出更澎湃的激情。

图文的记载不是将热爱封存在纸张之上，而是发出号召，我们要像爱惜自己的生命一样，保护并传承好历史文化遗产，让人们坚定文化自信，增强家国情怀，同时也记住乡愁，让古城的记忆永远流传。

这便是保定地域文化的时代书写。

New Chapters of the Regional Culture of Baoding

The ancient city is the root and soul of the people of Baoding, and the regional culture is its most attractive place.

With a history of more than 2,000 years, Baoding has left many immortal cultural imprints and has become a symbol of unique local customs. In the torrent of time, the historical and cultural heritage such as ancient pavilions and towers, inherited handicrafts, and fragrant local flavors have been regarded as treasures and carefully cared for by generations of Baoding people. Instead of disappearing with time, they are well deposited in the body of the ancient city and become a shining part of it.

One of the most direct ways to understand a city's regional culture is to read the city's newspaper. As the most authoritative and influential mainstream media in Baoding, Baoding Daily shoulders the responsibility of enhancing cultural identity and improving cultural self-confidence.

The year of 2019 marks the 70th anniversary of the founding of the

People's Republic of China. *Baoding Daily* launches a well-organized campaign that aims at telling Baoding stories and promoting regional culture through a series of reports as a celebration of the 70th anniversary of the founding of the People's Republic of China. A total of over one hundred reports are published and delivered in various media, and later published as a collection of books. By employing ways peculiar to media workers, we wake up stories deep hidden in history and explore new forms and routes to write and promote Baoding. The historical glory, cultural charm and the pulse of the times conveyed by these stories not only symbolize and arouse our pride, but also stand for a force that guides and inspires us to forge ahead.

The regional culture of the ancient city Baoding is so rich and profound that it could never be fully demonstrated in a book. As the second volume of the series, this book, based on the continuation of the style of the previous work, tells about the "past and present" of Baoding's regional cultural symbols such as Huai Army Office, Ancient Lotus Pond, and Tianshui Bridge. Having witnessed tremendous changes in the city with time passing by, Baoding culture becomes an integration of poems and faraway places. Now, with the construction of a modern city with high-quality life in full swing, Baoding is writing its new stories, which, under people's protection and with their own rejuvenation, will better highlight the quality life in the city.

In line with the original intention and mission of carrying forward excellent traditional culture, we have been observing and thinking while recording the past and present of the city and predicting its future. We keep telling Baoding stories and conveying Baoding voices via news-style cultural proses. We hope to convey this strong humanistic feeling to more people, whether they are travelers from afar, visiting guests, or people who have read these words accidentally, they can all feel the profound connotation of Baoding culture.

Though it has been changing, the ancient city always remains young. Its living culture, inheriting the same spirit from its genes and nurtured by the fertile land of the culture of Baoding, exhibits the power of growth, vigor and vitality. Its passion is further unleashed by the "freshness" injected by this era.

We record stories in pictures and words not to seal our deep love for culture in the paper, but to call for efforts to cherish the historical and cultural heritage of our city as our lives and to pass them down. Our goal is to boost people's confidence in Chinese culture and love for our country, to let hometown memory take roots in people's minds and to retain memories of ancient cities.

This is a new chapter of Baoding regional culture.

目录

CONTENTS

南风北韵筑百年淮军公所

韩雁 刘澜

保定古城区西南隅，商业闹市一侧，层层民居深处，一片正在修缮的清代古建筑群引得路人侧目关注，尤其是青砖灰瓦砌成的马头墙高大耸立，尽显徽派建筑风貌。

绝大多数保定人都知道，这一片叫“淮军公所”，其附近小区也因此得名。居民们天天路过，盼着这片古建筑群早日露真颜。

2019年11月19日，作为施工负责人的安徽人魏大勇轻车熟路来到淮军公所正在修复的大戏楼旁，开始一天的工作。虽然专业从事徽派建筑修复工作多年，见多识广，但他仍不觉赞叹：“单讲规模，我至今还没见过比它宏大的徽派古戏楼。”

淮军公所修缮一期、二期工程已经完工，戏楼修缮是三期工程，计划2020年10月左右完工。

已修葺完毕的淮军公所正门在冬日阳光下静谧肃穆。着眼细节，备感其与众不同——徽派祠堂式牌楼门，设有左、中、右三个券门，冠北方官式歇山顶，其上镌刻“敕建李文忠公祠”。朱门影壁，仿佛隔绝了外界嘈杂喧闹，瞬间将人带入百年时空。

清代中期以后，作为直隶首府的保定成为天下官宦客商出入京城的重要门户和立足点，各省会馆云集。会馆又称为公所，大都具备公祭、演剧、乡亲寄宿等多种功能。晚清重臣李

淮军公所正门

鸿章修建的淮军公所，不仅成为其所率淮军及亲属迎来送往的招待处所，更兼具政治功能。

史载，淮军公所全称“保定淮军昭忠祠暨公所”。1870年李鸿章奉旨率淮军至保定任直隶总督，于1888年修建昭忠祠和祭场，1891年竣工。1901年李鸿章死后，部分建筑改为李鸿章祠。这是继无锡等地之后，李鸿章建造的第五所淮军昭忠祠，其见证了晚清历史上的淮军兴衰、直隶风云及李鸿章宦海沉浮。

“依据现存建筑、史料、走访调查和勘探发掘，淮军公所占地在26 666平方米以上，古建筑面积5000多平方米，分为李鸿章专祠、昭忠祠、祠堂管理办公区、公所院、杂役区、操场、荷花塘及花园8个区域。”韩存到淮军公所管理所工作时间不长，但对这里

李鸿章专祠正殿

的感情随着了解的加深而愈发深厚，“听老人们叨念，当年这里修建时引得南北工匠同台竞秀，在施工中各自争奇斗巧，力显其能，结果把这座大院建得南北风韵合璧不俗……”

穿过迎宾院、二进院，看罢专祠正殿，步入一条东西走向的甬道，能清晰感受到：一巷之隔，南边是马头墙、透风脊，券门、柱石、梁架“无处不雕花”，精巧秀美，门楣檐下的墨线画清淡简雅；北部是四合院，硬山顶、清水脊、槅扇门、棂花等式样古朴厚重。南工择石材防潮，北匠取木材防起碱……南北相望，两种建筑风格与工艺相得益彰。

别具一格的垂花月亮门最能展现徽派“三雕”之精美：飞檐翘角，花篮垂柱，倒挂楣子满刻花鸟，砖石木构件雕刻得精巧入微，

垂花月亮门

尤其一对透雕狮子滚绣球玲珑剔透……

从1984年被列为保定市重点文物保护单位，1991年被国家建设部、文化部公布为中国近现代优秀建筑，1993年成为河北省文物保护单位，到2013年5月被国务院列为全国重点文物保护单位，淮军公所独有的历史文化价值愈发突出。

“中华人民共和国成立后，淮军公所曾被各类学校、机关等占用。”淮军公所管理所综合业务部主任王玮说，“虽然房屋几经易主，但很多绘画和雕刻都得以保留，特别是戏楼，所见留存令人欣喜。等戏楼修复好，可以像天津广东会馆戏楼一样建成戏剧博物馆……”

一批批历史学与建筑学专家、学者，以及曾经住在附近的居民挂念着这里，除了慨叹这座百年建筑承载的多重历史文化内涵，更对其修复、保护和利用寄托深情厚望。

保定职业技术学院副教授杜卫民积极推进产教融合，引导院校学生将毕业设计与收集并梳理淮军公所史料档案、做好布展宣传相结合。他说：“城市建筑遗迹被称为‘无言史书’‘凝固的乐章’，除了做好修缮保护工作，更重要的是今后如何让文物‘活’起来，让年轻人参与进来，更好地将文化传承下去……”

（历史文化顾问：直隶总督署吴蔚）

The Featured Century-old Huai Army Office

Han Yan Liu Lan

In the southwest of the old town in Baoding, hidden in all buildings, a complex of ancient buildings of the Qing Dynasty under renovation seems quite special, especially the towering horse-head wall made of blue bricks and gray tiles, showing the features of Hui-style Building.

Most people in Baoding know that this area is called "Huai Army Office", and the neighborhood is named after it. Residents pass by every day, looking forward to the early appearance of this ancient building complex.

On November 19, 2019, Wei Dayong, who is in charge of the construction, came to the grand theater building, which was being repaired at Huai Army Office, and started his day's work. Although he has been professionally engaged in the restoration of Hui-style architecture for many years and is knowledgeable, he exclaimed in admiration: "In terms of the scale, I have not seen an ancient Hui-style theater bigger than it."

The phase-1 and phase-2 renovation projects of Huai Army Office have been completed, and renovation of the theatrical building is the 3rd phase project, which is planned to be completed around October 2020.

The main gate of the repaired Huai Army Office is quiet and solemn in the winter sun. Focusing on the details, we can feel its uniqueness—The Hui-style archway gate for the ancestral shrine has three arched doors on the left, middle and right; on top of the gate is a gable and hip roof with a typical official style in the north, on which are engraved characters “Ancestral Shrine of Li Wenzhong Built by Imperial Order”. It feels as if the red gate and screen wall has completely isolated the place from external noise, bringing visitors instantly back to hundreds of years ago.

After the mid-Qing Dynasty, Baoding, as the capital of Zhili Province, became an important gateway and foothold for for officials and businessmen to visit the capital, and provincial guilds gathered. Guild halls, also known as guild buildings, most have multiple functions such as public memorial services, theatrical performances and accommodation for locals. The Huai Army Office built by Li Hongzhang, an important Minister of the late Qing Dynasty, not only became a reception place for his Huai Army and his relatives, but also had political functions.

According to historic records, the full name of Huai Army Office is “Baoding Huai Army Zhaozhong Ancestral Shrine and Guild Building”. In 1870, Li Hongzhang led the Huai Army to Baoding as governor of Zhili. The Zhaozhong Shrine were built by Li Hongzhang in 1870. The Sacrificial Venue were built by Li Hongzhang in 1888, and the construction were completed in 1891. This is the fifth Huai Army Zhaozhong Shrine built by him, after those in Wuxi and other places. It has witnessed the rise and fall of the Huai Army, major events in Zhili Province and ups and downs of Li Hongzhang in the history of the late Qing dynasty.

“According to the existing buildings, historical materials, visits and surveys, and exploration and excavations, the Huai Army Office covers an area of more than 26,666 square meters, and the ancient building area is more than 5,000 square meters. It is divided into eight areas: Li Hongzhang Temple, Loyalty Memorial Temple, ancestral hall management office area, office yard, miscellaneous service area, playground, lotus pond and flower garden.” Han Cun has not worked long in the management office of Huai Army Office, but his feelings for this place have grown deeper as his understanding deepens. “As was told by the old people, when it was built, it attracted the craftsmen from the North and the South, who competed on the same stage here. The construction of the Huai Army Office also initiated a race between architectural craftsmen in northern and southern China, who competed to contribute their creativity to the ingenious courtyard integrating styles from both north and south.

After walking through the Guest-greeting Yard and the Second Yard and appreciating the main hall of the shrine, you will arrive at an east-west aisle that gives you a clear perception of distinctive landscapes separated by it: the south are full of exquisite and beautiful carved patterns on corbel gables, drafty ridges, arched doors, pillars and beam mounts, as well as elegant and simplistic ink drawings on eaves lintel; in the north is a quadrangle teeming with patterns in ancient fashion on gabbled roofs, clear water ridges, partition doors and frames. The southern craftsmen adopted stone materials for purpose of damp-proof, while their northern counterparts chose wood materials to prevent alkalization, demonstrating architectural styles and techniques that perfectly echo each other.

The unique full-moon-shaped festoon door is the best example of the exquisiteness of the "three Hui-style carvings", including overhanging eaves, columns with hanging baskets of flowers, inverted lintels covered with engraved flowers and birds, delicately engravings on brick, stone and wood components, and particularly, a pair of hollowed-out carvings of lions sporting with an embroidered ball...

In 1984, it was listed as the key cultural relics protection unit of Baoding City. In 1991, it was announced as the Outstanding Architecture of Modern China by the Ministry of Construction and the Ministry of Culture. It became a cultural relics protection unit in Hebei Province in 1993, and was listed as a national key cultural relics protection unit by the State Council in May 2013. The unique historical and cultural value of Hua Army Office has become increasingly prominent.

"After the founding of the People's Republic of China, the Huai Army Office was occupied by all kinds of schools and agencies." Wang Wei, director of the comprehensive business department of the Huai Army Office, said, "Although its owners has changed several times, many paintings and carvings have survived, especially the opera house. When it is restored, it can be built into a theater museum just like the Guangdong Theater Building in Tianjin..."

A group of history and architecture experts, scholars, as well as former residents are concerned about this place. In addition to lamenting the multiple historical and cultural connotations carried by this century-old building, they also place deep hopes on its restoration, protection and utilization...

Du Weimin, associate professor of Baoding Vocational and Technical College, actively promoted the integration of industry and education, and guided students to combine the graduation project with the collection and sorting of historical records of Huai Army Office and the promotion of the exhibition. "Urban architectural relics are known as 'silent history' and 'frozen music'," he said. "In addition to good renovation and protection, what is more important is how to make cultural relics 'alive' in the future, to let young people participate in the better transmission of culture..."

(Consultant on History and Culture:
Wu Wei from Zhili Governor's Office)

一种味道飘香百年
——探寻保定老字号『白家罩饼』

张洁

荷叶饼撕成寸大的云彩形铺在最底层，卤制好的牛肉切成薄片覆盖在上面，点缀些绿白相间的葱丝，再用滚烫的老汤多次浇盖后，一份牛肉罩饼就上桌了。

相传清朝年间，嘉庆皇帝南巡路过保定，忽然闻到诱人的香味，便问左右香气从何而来。陪同官员将路边小摊的牛肉罩饼呈上，皇帝品尝过后称赞："色、香、味俱佳。"由此，保定的牛肉罩饼声名远扬。

说起保定的牛肉罩饼，"老保定"一定会推荐老字号"白家罩饼"。2019年11月20日12时，正是午饭时段，记者走进"白家罩饼"老店，探寻这延续了近百年、凝聚了四代人心血的牛肉罩饼为何受到人们的喜爱。

刚一进店，就看见伙计端着刚出锅的罩饼从身旁经过，一阵肉香迎面扑来，忍不住让人连吸几口香气。

在后厨操作间，记者见到了大厨白刚，他看上去30多岁，是这家老字号的第四代接班人，那手艺是祖传的。

灶台上，一大盘切好的牛肉片薄厚均匀、色诱人。

"要想做出好的牛肉罩饼，肉的用料必须讲究。"白刚介绍，"我们指定专人采购上等陕西黄牛回来，由清真寺的掌教屠宰，最后选用中肋和腱子肉为原材料。牛肉出锅，就连切功也是学问，每一刀都要将纹理切断，否则牛肉嚼在嘴里会发硬、咬不断。”

俗话说：“唱戏的腔，厨师的汤。”有了浓郁鲜香的汤，才有好吃的牛肉罩饼。只见后厨里，一口直径一米多的大锅里汤汁翻滚，不停冒着热气，白刚上前舀起一勺浓汤说：“这可是镇店之宝，店里煮汤遵从套汤古法，每天都要留一桶底汤以供次日使用，老汤已延续了40多年，从未间断过。”

看似简单的一锅汤，使用的香料居然有30多种。见记者有些吃惊，白刚拿出一包新料包，调料为粉状，约200克。白刚说：“祖上传下来的料包是直接把所有香料包在一起，有两个巴掌大小，一包熬制六锅牛肉。传到我这里进行了改进，把调料磨成粉并分装，一次一包，用着方便还更好出味儿。”

除了牛肉，饼也是至关重要的食材之一，“白家罩饼”用的是荷叶饼。什么是荷叶饼？就是面饼烙出来有荷叶大小，两层，与荷叶薄厚无异，因此得名。

饼有特点，入盘也有独到之处——面饼必须手撕，来回平搓后再装盘。这为何？白刚解释道：“顺着面筋撕出来的饼口感更好，来回平搓把饼分层打散，才更容易入味儿。”

最后一道工序是浇汤。大锅的上面架着架子，占据了锅面一半的位置，牛肉和饼摆盘放在上面就开始浇汤。浇盖次数在于制作师傅对于面饼形态的把握，行话叫作“浇几手”，直到面饼筋道而不绵软为止。也有例外，碰上年岁大的顾客，师傅会根据顾客的需求多浇几遍，使饼更软。

40岁的郎宏业家住“白家罩饼”饭店附近，是店里的老顾客，他对“白家罩饼”情有独钟：“打小就吃他家的牛肉罩饼，就好这

撕饼

浇汤

口儿。”看着他吃得甚是满足，记者也忍不住捧上一碗尝尝鲜。筋道的面饼裹挟着馥郁的香气，红润的牛肉肥而不腻，再连啜几口浓汤下肚，甭提有多舒坦。

延伸阅读：“白家罩饼”简介

“白家罩饼”由白络春老人创办。白络春起初在保定本地的饭庄当学徒，出徒后到石家庄中和轩饭庄积累经验，后几经周折，于1923年在山西太原开了一家饭庄，利用在中和轩饭庄学得的牛肉罩饼技艺并结合自身感悟，专门经营“老白牛肉罩饼”。

白络春的儿子白桂森自小跟随父亲，耳濡目染也喜欢上了勤行，经过多年的磨砺，煎、炒、烹、炸样样精通。白桂森先后在山西潞安府、陕西西安经营“老白牛肉罩饼”。20世纪50年代，公私合营后，白桂森带着家人返回保定的农村老家。

改革开放后，党的惠民政策又使白桂森产生了重操旧业的想法。1977年，白桂森在保定南河坡开了一家牛肉罩饼店，并将店名“白家罩饼”进行注册。小店开业后，白桂森在父亲传授的配方基础上加以改进，调制出独特的配方。

“白家罩饼”几十年如一日始终保持自己的独特风味，成为保定家喻户晓的老字号饭店。

One flavor, Scent of Hundred Years

—Baoding's Famous Brand "Bai's Zhaobing"

Zhang Jie

The lotus leaf flatbread is torn into inch-large cloud shapes and spread on the bottom layer. The marinated beef is sliced and covered on top, dotted with some green and white scallions, and then poured and covered with scalding soup for several times, a Beef Zhaobing (Beef over Flatbread) is served on the table.

An anecdote has it that during the Qing Dynasty, Emperor Jiaqing suddenly sensed some appetizing smell when passing by Baoding in his southward tour. He then asked his entourage where the scent came from. An accompanying official presented Beef Zhaobing (Beef over Flatbread) to the emperor. After taking a bite, the emperor praised that it was "perfect in color, aroma and taste." As a result, Baoding's Beef Zhaobing became famous.

Speaking of Baoding's Beef Zhaobing, local people will definitely recommend the time-honored "Bai's Zhaobing". At 12 o'clock on November 20, 2019, it was lunchtime. As a reporter, I also paid a personal visit to the time-honored restaurant "Bai's Zhaobing" to explore the secret behind the popularity of the Beef Zhaobing which has been passed down across four generations.

As soon as I entered the restaurant, a waiter was passing by me, serving a freshly-made Zhaobing. I instantly perceived a pleasant smell of tender and tasty beef.

In the kitchen of the restaurant, I met chef Bai Gang. He seemed in his early 30s and is the 4th-generation inheritor of the time-honored brand. In other words, the recipe of the signature food was actually invented by his ancestors.

On the countertop was a large plate of evenly sliced beef that looked very appealing.

"To make good Beef Zhaobing, you must be careful with the quality of the meat," said Bai, "we have designated staff responsible for purchasing high-quality beef of yellow cattle from Shaanxi. The cattle were personally slaughtered by the leader of a mosque, and we only select the cut in the midrib area and shank as our main ingredient. Even slicing the beef after it is cooked is an intricate skill. The grain of the beef must be severed in each cut, otherwise, it will be too chewy. "

As the saying goes, "what soup means to a chef is just like what tones to an opera performer." Only with the full-bodied, fresh soup can Beef Zhaobing become delicious. In the kitchen, the hot and steaming soup was rolling in the huge wok with a diameter of over 1 meter. Scooping up the thick soup, Bai said, "This is arguably the most precious thing in this restaurant. Every day we leave a bucket of base soup for the next day. In this way, the soup has been continuously used and renewed for over 40 years without stopping."

It is unimaginable that the seemingly simple soup contains more than 30 spices. Perceiving the surprised look of me, Bai Gang took out a new bag of powdered spices which weighed around 200g. He said, "The spice bag, which is also passed down from my ancestors, is prepared by directly mixing all spices. One bag is no bigger than two palms and enough for stewing 6 woks of beef. When the restaurant was handed over to me, I made some improvements to the spice bag. I grind these spices into powder and reduce its size to just being enough for one-pot cooking. It is both convenient and easy to drive the flavors out."

In addition to beef, flatbread is also one of the most important ingredients.

"Bai's Zhaobing" uses lotus leaf flatbread. What is lotus leaf flatbread? The flatbread got its the name as they are baked in the size of lotus leaves, with two layers, which are as thin as the lotus leaves.

The flatbread has its own characteristics, and there is a unique way to put it on the plate - the flatbread must be torn by hand, rubbed flat back and forth before being put on the plate. Why is this? Bai Gang explained: "The flatbread tastes better when it is torn out along the gluten. It is easier to absorb the flavor of the flatbread by rubbing it back and forth and break it up in layers."

The last procedure will be "pouring the soup". A shelf is sitting on the pot, covering half of the pot. Soup will be poured on the beef and flatbread. The number of pouring is determined by the chef, he will continue to pour until the flatbread is chewy but not soft. Exceptions happen to the elders since the chef will pour more times to make it softer.

Lang Hongye, in his 40s, lives near the restaurant selling the Bai's Zhao bing, and he is a regular guest here. He said, "I have eaten his flatbread since I was a little kid, I'm just addicted to it." The reporter cannot resist having one after seeing him enjoy his flatbread. Eating the chewy flatbread with thick flavor, tender beef, and sips of soup, how comfortable it is!

Extended Reading: Introduction to "Bai's Zhaobing"

"Bai's Zhaobing" was founded by the elderly Bai Luochun. Bai Luochun first worked as an apprentice in a local restaurant in Baoding. After his apprenticeship, he went to Zhonghexuan Restaurant in Shijiazhuang to accumulate experience. After many setbacks, In 1923, he opened a restaurant in Taiyuan, Shanxi Province. By combining the Beef Zhaobing preparation skills he learned at Zhonghexuan Restaurant with his personal thoughts, he started his own business named "Laobai Beef Zhaobing".

Bai Guisen, the son of Bai Luochun, had followed his father ever since his childhood and gradually developed an interest in the catering trade. Over years of practice, he became proficient in various cooking skills such as pan-frying, stir-frying, stewing and deep-frying. Bai Guisen operated his "Laobai

Beef Zhaobing" business successively in Lu'an Fu, Shanxi Province and Xi'an, Shanxi Province. After the joint state-private ownership reform in the 1950s, Bai Guisen returned to his rural hometown along with his family.

The implementation of the reform and opening-up and other beneficial policies prompted Bai Guisen to restart his business. In 1977, Bai Guisen opened a Zhaobing shop in Nanhepo, Baoding, and registered the name "Bai's Zhaobing". After the store opened, Bai Guisen improved on the recipe taught by his father and formulated a unique recipe.

"Bai's Zhaobing" has maintained its own unique flavor for decades, and has become a well-known time-honored restaurant in Baoding.

清西陵桥群：见证一代代帝王的兴盛与寂寥

李凯丽　霍若雯　杨洪光

一座清西陵，半部清王史。清西陵位于保定市易县永宁山下，不仅是清代最后一处帝王陵墓群，也是现存规模宏大、保存最完整、陵寝建筑类型最齐全的古代皇室陵墓群。2019年10月30日，记者走进清西陵景区，探访这里一座座具有代表性的石桥。

泰陵是清西陵的首陵，它占据了永宁山下最佳的位置，是清西陵中修建最早、规模最大的陵寝，无论在选址还是规划布局上，都是雍正年间繁荣与稳定的写照，其桥梁在清西陵49座桥中也最具意义。

步上神道，进入泰陵陵区的第一座建筑——五孔石拱桥。它坐落于北易水河之上，由青白石建成，平整厚重，雕有桃形望柱和荷叶净瓶栏板。桥长84.5米，宽8.7米，如飞虹跨溪般壮观。结伴同行的游客们站在桥上远眺，轻抚石栏，苍松巨柏，易水寒流。

“与清东陵不同，清西陵陵寝的第一个建筑都是以桥开始。”在景区工作了20年的清西陵保护区管理委员会资料室馆员冀艳明介绍，“在清西陵众多古桥中，泰陵五孔石拱桥的地位和意义非同一般。站在桥上环顾四周，桥下易水潺潺，莲叶田田，岸边古松郁郁葱葱，远处永宁山延绵起伏，红墙黄瓦隐映其间。陵寝中桥梁的作用，一是使整个建筑群紧凑而不松

泰陵的五孔石拱桥

散，渲染出庄严肃穆的氛围；二是使景观错落有致，有层次感，达到移步换景的效果。”

五孔石拱桥可谓景区的“明星桥”，乾隆帝曾39次踏上此桥。相传在这座桥上发生过一件趣事，乾隆祭祖行至五孔桥上，出一上联：“五孔桥，桥五孔，五孔桥上观五孔，五孔五孔五孔桥。”机智的刘墉马上跪在乾隆面前，对出了下联：“万岁爷，爷万岁，万岁爷前呼万岁，万岁万岁万万岁。”乾隆听后哈哈大笑，称刘墉是天下奇才。

在1986年电视剧版《西游记》中，唐太宗送别唐三藏的镜头就

泰陵的七孔石拱桥

是在泰陵拍摄的。唐三藏骑白马在五孔石拱桥上转身回望唐太宗，由此踏上了西天取经之路。

沿着神道继续前行，记者踏上了清西陵最长的一座桥，也是泰陵的第三座桥，即坐落在大碑楼和石像生之间的七孔石拱桥。它全长107米，宽9.05米，宏大的规模、完美的结构，在古代桥梁史上也是屈指可数的。行至桥上，记者看到相比五孔桥，七孔桥桥面的石板多有损坏，缝隙大，部分缺损严重的石板上标记了数字。

提到陵区内桥梁的维护修缮，冀艳明说："这些约300年前的石材大多是产自北京房山的青白石，非常坚固，且保养较好，整体上没有大修过，仅个别桥做过修缮。近期，景区将对七孔石拱桥酥

泰陵的三路三孔桥

碱严重的桥面条石、牙子石和如意石进行修缮。”

泰陵的最后一座桥是三路三孔桥，位于泰陵神道碑亭南侧，是这里规格最高的一座桥。其结构仿照故宫金水桥形式修建，寓意视死如生。作为主体建筑，桥上雕有龙凤望柱头。三路三孔桥的走法颇为讲究，从神道碑亭一侧看，左侧为君路，右侧为臣路，中间为神路。

离开泰陵，记者一行驱车向西，来到清代所有帝陵中最小的一座——慕陵。慕陵的三路三孔桥是清西陵中最特殊的一座，中间为一路拱桥，两侧均为平桥。

沿着这一座座青白石桥一路走来，人们就像亲手抚摸了清王朝

慕陵的三路三孔桥

的年轮，所思所见可能各有不同。

延伸阅读：清西陵形式多样的桥

古代陵寝建筑，非常注重对水的处理，陵区“所有随桥泊岸，酌量地势修理”。各式大小桥梁，随水脉而建，有水就要有桥，因此，陵寝的桥数量很多。清西陵内共有石桥49座，大多集中在4个帝陵之中，分布在各个陵寝的神道上，是神道穿过易水河、马漕沟的通道。这些桥形式多样，根据结构特点，可分为拱桥、平桥。拱桥中又有三孔桥、五孔桥、七孔桥，单路桥、三路桥，栏板桥、无栏板桥。平桥有29座，拱桥有20座。根据身份的不同，陵寝内桥的规模、数量也不尽相同，彰显了森严的封建等级制度。

Bridge Cluster at Western Qing Tombs: To Witness the Rise and Fall of Emperors

Li Kaili Huo Ruowen Yang Hongguang

The building of Western Qing Tombs represents half history of Qing Emperors.

Western Qing Tombs are located at the foot of Yongning Mountain, Yi County, Baoding City. It is the last royal mausoleums of the Qing Dynasty, and also the largest, the best preserved ancient royal mausoleums, featuring the most complete types of mausoleum buildings. On October 30, 2019, the reporter walked into the Western Qing Tombs scenic spot and visited the representative stone bridges here.

Tailing, also known as Tai Mausoleum, is the primary tomb among the Western Qing Tombs. It occupies the best position at the foot of Yongning Mountain, and was the earliest built and largest tomb of all. It is a portrayal of prosperity and stability during Emperor Yongzheng's reign in terms of site selection, planning and layout. Its bridges are also the most significant among the 49 bridges in the Western Qing Tombs.

Walking along the entryway towards the shrine, one would encounter the first structure in the Tailing area - the five-arch stone bridge. Stretching across the North Yishui River, the bridge was built of grey-white marble arranged in a flattened and stately manner. On the bridge are engraved peach-shaped railing posts and lotus-leaf-shaped vases on parapet panels. Measuring 84.5 meters long and 8.7 meters wide, the bridge magnificently stretches over the river like a rainbow. It is quite a scene to see when tourists stand on the bridge and look into the distance at the sturdy pines and giant cypresses, as well as the rolling Yishui River, with their hands gently holding the stone balustrades.

"Unlike the Eastern Qing Tombs, the first building in the Western Qing Tombs starts with a bridge." Ji Yanming, the librarian of the reference room of the Management Committee of the Western Qing Tombs Protected Area, who has worked in the scenic spot for 20 years, said, "Among the many ancient bridges in the Western Qing Tombs, the five-arch ston bridge of Tai Ling occupies an extraordinary place. Standing on the bridge and looking around, water flows under, the lotus grows, and pine prospers. In the distance, the Yongning Mountain stretches, and houses with red walls and yellow tiling are hidden. Bridge in the Emperor's resting place has two functions, one is to make the buildings more compact, giving a sense of solemnity, and another is to create a sense of spacing and depth, realizing the effect of different views at each turn."

The five-arch stone bridge is the star bridge of the scenic spot, Emperor Qianlong stepped on this bridge 39 times. An anecdote has it that an interesting thing happened to the bridge. In his trip to hold the ancestor-worship ceremony, Emperor Qianlong passed by the five-arch stone bridge and offered the first line of the couplet: "The five-arch stone bridge has five arches. Standing on the five-arch bridge to appreciate the five arches, five five five arch bridges." Hearing this, the witty official Liu Yong immediately kneeled in front of Qianlong and offered his second line: "Your lord of ten-thousand years will live ten thousand years. Humbly wishing your lord to live ten-thousand years, ten-thousand ten-thousand ten-thousand years." Qianlong burst into laughter upon hearing this, joking that Liu Yong was a genius.

In the 1986 version TV series *Journey to the West*, the scene in which the Emperor Taizong of Tang bids farewell to Tang Sanzang was shot in the Tailing area. The most famous shot in the scene depicts Tang Sanzang, riding the white horse on the five-arch stone bridge, looking back at Emperor Taizong

石柱上雕有精美图案

of Tang, setting off on his journey to the west.

Walking further along the sacred way, the reporter set foot on the longest bridge in the Western Qing Tombs, the third bridge in the Tailing area, which is a seven-arch stone bridge located between Dabei Tower and stone statues. It is 107 meters long and 9.05 meters wide. Its grand scale and perfect structure are rarely seen in the history of ancient bridges. Walking on the bridge, I realized that compared with the five-arch stone bridge, this bridge suffers much damage on stone plates of its surface, with numbers marked on part of badly damaged plates.

Referring to the maintenance and renovation of bridges in the mausoleum area, Ji Yanming said: “The stones about 300 years ago are mostly bluish white stones from Fangshan in Beijing. They are very strong and well maintained. Recently, the tourist zone replaced and repaired badly-cracked ashlars, curbs and ornamental stones on the seven-arch stone bridge. ”

The last bridge in the Tailing area is the three-way three-arch bridge located in the south of the Stele Pavilions of Tailing, which is also of the

石桥一侧

highest grade. A similar structure to that of the Golden Water Bridge of the Palace Museum is adopted to convey the idea of serving the dead as they would have served them alive. As the main structure of the bridge, railing post columns is carved with dragon and phoenix sculptures on the top. There is a sophisticated rule governing how one should walk through the three-way three-arch bridge: looking away from the Stele Pavilions, one could find that the imperial path on the left, the courtier path on the right and the divine path in the middle.

Leaving the Tailing area, reporters drove westward and came to the Muling—the smallest mausoleum among the Western Qing Tombs. The three-way three-arch bridge is arguably the most special bridge in Muling, which comprises an arched bridge in the middle and two flat bridges on both sides.

Walking across these bluish-white marble bridges elicits a feeling as if you have been given an opportunity to touch the annual rings of the Qing dynasty, giving rise to a diversity of perceptions.

Extended Reading: Varions Bridges in Western Qing Tombs

In ancient times, the imperial mausoleum architecture attached great importance to the treatment of water. In the mausoleum area, "all bridges and mooring quays were built with a consideration of local terrain". Various sized bridges were built along the water vein; wherever there is water, there are bridges. Thus, there exist a large number of bridges in the imperial mausoleum area. There is a total of 49 stone bridges in the Western Qing Tombs, most of which are distributed along the divine paths of the 4 imperial mausoleum areas, serving as passages of the divine paths across the Yishui River and Macaogou River. Adopting a variety of forms, these bridges can be roughly divided into arched and flat bridges based on structures. Arched bridges also include three-arch bridges, five-arch bridges, seven-arch bridges, one-way bridges, three-way bridges, parapet panel bridges and bridges without parapet panels. There are 29 flat bridges and 20 arched ones. Depending on their identities, the scale and number of inner bridges in the mausoleums are varied, reflecting the strict hierarchy of the feudal society.

保定邮路漫漫3000年

米冬冬 李娜 贾楠 于振涛

“你知道金台驿街这个名字的由来吗？清代光绪年间，保定馆驿金台驿就在金台驿街。现在管驿街小学的位置是北宋建隆年间金台驿站的初址，当时叫‘金台顿’。”保定市集邮协会副会长、保定市邮电局经营管理部原主任马天迪向记者讲述了保定邮政的“前世今生”。

金台驿街距离现在的保定邮政公司只有450米。历史的车轮漫漫，如今的金台驿街已找不到当年驿站的旧址，我们只能在史料中感受“光明眩目，过如飞电，望之者无不避路”的古代邮驿打马飞奔传信的场景。

古代通信是近代邮电通信的起源，保定在周朝就建立了专为官府传递文书的邮驿组织。明末清初，保定境内设有驿站18处、驿铺168处。在民间，传递私人书缄的保定民信局前身创立于清乾隆十六年（1751），至1907年，保定的民信局已有11处，大部分设置在当时的西门内二道口，邮件传递在民信局中后期主要通过铁路运输实现。

保定的古代邮驿、民信局从开设到衰落，历经3000多年。因保定历代曾置州、府、省会，以军事、政治、文化城市著称，因此邮驿、民信局不仅建立早且网络密布，在全国首屈一指，镌刻下保定邮史上引人注目的篇章。

清雍正二年（1724）至民国初期，保定为直隶总督署所在地。由于军事需要，清光绪

保定金台驿旧址（管驿街）

十一年（1885），架设了保定至天津的有线电报线路；光绪十三年（1887），设立了保定电报局。

光绪二十五年（1899），在保定城内关帝庙，保定大清邮政成立。它是保定邮政局的前身，也是保定近代邮政的开端。

1912年，大清邮政改为“中华民国邮政”，保定邮政局分局改为“保定邮务局”。

抗日战争期间，保定于1937年沦陷，邮务局被日本人控制。中国共产党领导的革命武装先后在阜平、唐县、曲阳、涞源等地建立了交通邮政组织。1937年，中国共产党在阜平陈庄创办了晋察冀边区临时邮政，发行了油印版第一组邮票。1938年，唐县临时邮政发行的两枚木刻版“唐县临时邮票”在当前的集邮市场弥足珍贵。

1948年11月22日，保定解放，保定邮务局回到人民手中。中华人民共和国成立后，中国邮政事业翻开崭新的一页，邮政普遍服务“飞”入寻常百姓家。头戴绿色大檐帽、骑着绿色自行车的邮递员穿梭于城乡街巷，成为一道亮丽的风景线。

民国时期保定“广泰”民信局旧址（大金钱胡同）

1978年改革开放后，保定邮政通信事业全面振兴，形成了沟通城乡、覆盖全市、连通世界的现代邮政网络，实现了航空、铁路、公路、水路等多种运输手段的综合利用。

进入21世纪，伴随移动互联网的兴起和新技术的广泛应用，电子邮件、短信、微信等逐渐成为人们主要的通信方式，传统的邮政业务逐年衰落，“家书抵万金”的时代渐行渐远。据保定邮政市场营销部副主任董贵军介绍：“目前全市邮政网点达313个，投递道段822个，盈利的网点不足10%。地处边远山区的邮政网点，有的每月营业额只有几百元。邮政承担着为公众提供普遍服务的职能，网点普及率高且资费低廉，能最大限度满足百姓的通邮需求。只要邮政网络存在，普遍服务就不会消失。”

1998年，中国邮政事业迎来一项重大体制改革——邮政与电信分离。2006年8月，国务院批准实行“政企分开”政策，保定邮政局更名为“中国邮政集团公司保定市分公司”。同年，中国邮政储蓄银行保定市分行成立。2010年，中国邮政速递物流股份有限公司

清代北洋电报局保定分局旧址（北大街）

保定市分公司挂牌运营。传统邮政转型为现代邮政。

创新引领发展。近年来，保定邮政确立“一体两翼”战略，打造适应现代电子商务发展模式的线上线下为一体的综合便民服务平台，金融和寄递服务发展迅速。目前，保定邮政在全市城乡建立了金融网点136个，开展储蓄、代发、代缴等便民服务，其年收入占企业总收入的60%以上。近5年，邮政快递业务量每年递增50%。邮政“三农”服务网络日臻完善，累计建设邮乐购站点5333个，行政村覆盖率达98.14%，有效网点占比66.88%。2018年，保定邮政实现业务收入9.63亿元。

邮路漫漫3000年，见证着古城的发展。马天迪说：“保定这座历史文化名城有着悠久的邮政史。保定元素屡屡登上作为‘国家名片’的邮票，如成语故事‘鹬蚌相争’‘闻鸡起舞’，历史人物祖冲之，还有紫荆关长城、清泰陵、冉庄地道战纪念馆、保定中关村创新中心、雄县牌楼、容和塔、白洋淀、白洋淀高铁站等先后出现在邮票上，成为保定的骄傲。”

The 3,000 -year Postal History in Baoding

Mi Dongdong Li Na Jia Nan Yu Zhentao

"Do you know how Jintaiyi Street got its name? During Emperor Guangxu's reign of the Qing Dynasty, Baoding Jintaiyi station was located in Jintaiyi Street. The current location of Guanyi Street Primary School is the original site of Jintaiyi Post Station during the Jianlong period of the Northern Song Dynasty, which was then called Jintai Dun." Ma Tiandi, vice president of Baoding Philatelic Association and former director of the Operation and Management Department of Baoding Post and Telecommunications Bureau, told reporters about the "past life" of Baoding Post.

Jintaiyi Street is only 450 meters away from the present Baoding Post Office. As time passed, we can no longer find the old post house today, but only imagine the scene of "riding horse fast to send mails" through the historical records.

Ancient mail delivery is the origin of modern post and telecommunications. In the Zhou Dynasty, Baoding established post stations to deliver documents for the government. In the late Ming and early Qing Dynasties, there were 18 post stations and 168 post shops in Baoding. Among the people, the predecessor of Baoding civil post office, which delivered private letters, was founded in the 16th year of Emperor Qianlong of the Qing Dynasty (1751). By 1907, there were 11 civil post offices in Baoding, most of which were set at Erdaokou in the west gate at that time. Mail delivery was mainly conducted through railway transportation in the middle and late stages of the civil post office.

Baoding's ancient post station and civil post office have experienced more than 3, 000 years from its establishment to its decline. Since Baoding was once a state, government and provincial capital in the past dynasties, it is famous as a military, political and cultural city. The post station and civil post office network in Baoding were established quite early in history, among the first in China, and played prominent roles in Baoding's postal history.

From the second year of Emperor Yongzheng of the Qing Dynasty (1724) to the early period of the Republic of China, Baoding was the seat of the Zhili Governor's office. Due to military needs, a wired telegraph line from Baoding to Tianjin was built in the 11th year of Emperor Guangxu of the Qing Dynasty (1885); In the 13th year of Emperor Guangxu (1887), Baoding Telegraph Office was established.

In the 25th year of Emperor Guangxu (1899), Baoding Qing Post was established in Guandi Temple in Baoding City. It is the predecessor of Baoding Post Bureau and the beginning of Baoding modern postal industry.

In 1912, Qing Post turned into China Post, and Baoding Post Bureau was changed into Baoding Postal Service.

During the Anti-Japanese War, Baoding was occupied by the Japanese army in 1937, and the post office came under the Japanese control. The revolutionary armed forces led by the Communist Party of China have successively established transportation and postal organizations in Fuping, Tangxian, Quyang, Laiyuan and other places. In 1937, the Communist Party of China established the temporary postal service in the Shanxi-Chahar-Hebei Border Area in Chenzhuang, Fuping, and issued the first set of mimeographed stamps. In 1938, the two woodblock "Tangxian Temporary Stamps" issued by the Tangxian Temporary Post Office are very precious in the current philatelic market.

On November 22, 1948, Baoding was liberated, and the Baoding Post

Service returned to the hands of the people. After the founding of the PRC, the postal services of China Post have taken on a new road and entered the life of common people. People can always see a postman wearing a green wide grim hat, and riding a green bike to send mails on the streets.

After the reform and opening-up in 1978, post mail service in Baoding has been revitalized, and the modern post network connecting urban and rural areas, and covering all corners of the city and even the world has been built, realizing the comprehensive utilization of air, railway, highway and waterway transportation.

In the 21st century, with the rise of mobile Internet and the wide application of new technologies, e-mail, SMS and Wechat have gradually become people's main means of communication. The traditional postal service is declining year by year, and the era of "A letter from home is a priceless treasure" is gradually fading away. According to Dong Guijun, deputy director of the Marketing Department of Baoding Post: "At present, there are 313 postal outlets and 822 delivery sections in the city, with less than 10% profitable outlets. Some postal outlets located in remote mountainous areas have a monthly turnover of only a few hundred yuan. The postal service undertakes the function of providing universal services for the public. With high network penetration rate and low charges, which can meet people's demand for postal service to the greatest extent. As long as the postal network exists, universal services will not disappear."

In 1998, China's postal service ushered in a major institutional reform—the separation of postal services and telecommunications. In August 2006, the State Council approved the implementation of the policy of "separating government from enterprises", and Baoding Post Bureau was renamed "Baoding Branch of China Post Group Corporation". In the same year, the Baoding Branch of China Postal Savings Bank was established. In 2010, Baoding Branch of China Post Express and Logistics Co., Ltd. was put into operation. The traditional postal service is transformed into modern postal service.

Innovation drives development. In recent years, Baoding Post has adopted the strategy of "One Body Two Wings" to build a comprehensive online and offline public service platform adapted to modern e-commerce development mode. Financial and delivery services have developed rapidly. At present, Baoding Post has established 136 financial outlets in urban and rural areas of the city, providing convenient services such as savings, agency pay off and agency payment. Its annual income accounts for more than 60% of the total income of the enterprise. In the past five years, the volume of postal express industry increases by 50% every year. The postal service network for agriculture, rural areas and farmers is improving day by day, with a total of 5,333 Ule (Happy Post) outlets, covering 98.14% of administrative villages and accounting for 66.88% of effective outlets. In 2018, Baoding Post achieved business revenue of 963 million yuan.

The long postal route has witnessed the development of the ancient city for 3,000 years. Ma Tiandi said: "Baoding, a historical and cultural city, has a long postal history. Baoding elements have repeatedly been incorporated into the design of stamps, such as the well-known idiom stories "the fight between waterfowl and river mussel" and "rising upon the crowing of the rooster", the historical figure Zu Chongzhi, Tai Mausoleum of Qing Dynasty Zijingguan Great Wall, Ranzhuang Tunnel War Memorial Hall, Baoding Zhongguancun Innovation Center, Xiongxian Archway, Ronghe Tower, Baiyangdian Lake, Baiyangdian High-speed Railway Station. They have successively appeared on stamps and become the pride of Baoding."

涿州下胡良桥，400多年不大修的『桥坚强』

邸志永　范钊

桥洞上方的吞水兽

相比高端大气、奉旨重修的永济桥，在其两公里之外的下胡良桥，则显得更加朴素亲民。2019年10月23日，记者来到下胡良桥，桥面上晾晒的玉米、穿梭的行人，让这座445岁的古桥更加接地气。

正在桥上晒玉米的下胡良村村民翟贵山，对家门口的这座桥分外自豪："听我们村的老人讲，这座桥已有400多年，从来没有大修过。"

翟贵山的话，也得到涿州市文物保管所所长黄涿生的认可："这座桥可以说是永济桥的兄弟桥，也是万历二年（1574）宰相张居正主持修建的。400多年来，下胡良桥没有重建的历史记载，除了桥本身坚固之外，还有一个重要原因，胡良河源头为泉水，多年来水量不像拒马河那般大。"

记者了解到，下胡良桥一直是京畿要道，直到20世纪80年代末，桥的通行量逐渐减小，

2013年下胡良桥成为国保单位

但仍是出入下胡良村的通道之一。翟贵山称，虽然桥面改成了水泥路面，但桥两侧的护栏是400多年前留下来的。

在桥两侧，记者看到同永济桥相仿的吞水兽头，个别的兽头有些破损。在桥的石袱上，还有孩子们刻下的游戏印记。不过，相比永济桥精美的莲叶净瓶，下胡良桥栏板非常朴素，没有任何雕饰。

据《涿州县志》记载，胡良河宽约10米，上游多为泉水，泉水清澈冬不结冰，这在北方比较少见。作为京畿要道之一，下胡良桥不仅靠近涿州贡米产地，还以优美景色吸引着南来北往的人们。

记者在现场看到，胡良河的水量并不充沛，看上去还有些浑浊。此外，河道大部分被蒲草等水生植物占据，偶尔有水鸟飞出来。

“多年来，胡良河的水都不大。印象里上一次来大水，是在1986年，当时水都快要没到桥面，不过这座桥安然无恙。”翟贵山称。涿州八景之一的“胡良晓月”就在这里。不过，后来由于修路将一部分河水挡住，“胡良晓月”这一美景再也看不到了。

下胡良桥航拍图

对此，黄涿生并不认同，他说了“胡良晓月”另一个版本：天上有月亮时，黎明时分，雄鸡报晓，天色微明。在晨光熹微中，清清的河水静静流淌，水中映出一片残月，波光桥影情景交融，引人入胜。

2013年，下胡良桥成为全国重点文物保护单位。而今，桥两头设置了2.4米的限高设施，不过小车和行人依旧可通过，让这座古桥继续发挥它的功能。

对于下胡良桥的未来，黄涿生告诉记者，在下胡良桥西侧几公里处，便是涿州贡米的产地。根据《隋书·食货志》记载，涿州种植水稻已有1400多年历史。1973年，联合国粮农组织考察涿州时称，该地区为“得天独厚盛产水稻的好地方”。

黄涿生说：“未来，这里会打造成十八里稻香村，成为生态农业景区。我们计划将下胡良桥作为起点，游客们可以从这里下车步行，在参观桥之后，一路参观胡良河，欣赏两岸金黄的稻谷，体验

下胡良桥如今限高2.4米

涿州的生态、农业和厚重的历史文化。”

延伸阅读：下胡良桥简介

下胡良桥始建于明万历二年（1574），为单路五孔石拱桥。桥全长69米，桥面宽9.14米，由分水到桥面高4.43米，望柱头雕成方形卷叶，望柱高1.40米，栏板高0.81米。下胡良桥与拒马河上的永济桥同一年建造，都是古代京畿交通重要桥梁，具有很高的历史、科学和艺术价值。

Xiahuliang Bridge in Zhuozhou, the "Tough Bridge" with No Major Repairs for 400 Years

Di Zhiyong Fan Zhao

Compared with the high-grade Yongji Bridge rebuilt by the imperial verdict, the Xiahuliang Bridge located two kilometers away appears to be more simplistic and friendly. On October 23, 2019, the reporter came to Xiahuliang Bridge. The dried corn and shuttling pedestrians on the bridge deck made the 445-year-old bridge more grounded.

Zhai Guishan, a villager in Xiahuliang Village, who was drying corn on the bridge, was very proud of the bridge in front of his house: "According to the old people in our village, this bridge has been over 400 years old and has never been overhauled."

Zhai Guishan's words were also recognized by Huang Zhuosheng, director of the Zhuozhou City Cultural Relics Preservation Office: "This bridge can be said to be the 'brother bridge' of Yongji Bridge, and it was also built under the auspices of Prime Minister Zhang Juzheng in the second year of Emperor Wanli (1574). For more than 400 years, there is no historical record of the reconstruction of Xiahuliang Bridge. In addition to the solidity of the bridge itself, there is another important reason. The source of Huliang River is spring water, and the water volume has not been as large as the Juma River for many years."

The reporter learned that Xiahuliang Bridge has been a thoroughfare in the capital city and its environs until the end of the 1980s, the bridge traffic gradually decreased, but it is still one of the accesses to Xiahuliang Village. Zhai said that although the bridge was paved with cement, the guardrails on both sides of the bridge were left over from more than 400 years ago.

On both sides of the bridge, the reporter saw water-swallowing beast heads similar to Yongji Bridge, some of which were damaged. On the bridge, you can still see the marks left by the children when they played games. However, compared with the exquisite lotus leaf bottle of Yongji Bridge, the handrails of Xiahuliang Bridge are very simple, without any carving.

According to *Zhuozhou County Annals*, Huliang River is about 10 meters wide, and its upstream is mostly spring water. The spring water is clear and does not freeze in winter, which is rare in the north. As one of the thoroughfares in the capital city and its environs, Xiahuliang Bridge is not only close to the origin of Zhuozhou tribute rice, but also attracts people from south to north with its beautiful scenery.

The reporter saw that the water volume of Huliang river is not sufficient and looks turbid. In addition, most of the river is occupied by aquatic plants such as papyrus, and occasionally water birds fly out.

"Over the years, the water of Huliang river has not been large. In my impression, the last flood was in 1986. At that time, the water was about to reach the bridge deck, but the bridge was safe and sound." Zhai Guishan said. "Hu Liang Xiao Yue", one of the eight best views in Zhuozhou, is here. However, the beautiful scenery of "Hu Liang Xiao Yue" was never seen again due to the road construction that blocked part of the river.

However, Huang Zhuosheng held a different opinion, who provided another version of "Hu Liang Xiao Yue": when the moon is hanging in the sky at dawn, the rooster starts to crow as the sky is faintly light. Under the first faint rays of dawn, the clear water silently flows along the river, with a crescent moon reflected in the water. That, in combination with the shimmering waves

下胡良桥晾晒的玉米，让这座桥更接地气

and bridge reflection, gives rise to an appealing scene.

In 2013, Xiahuliang Bridge became a national key cultural relics protection unit. Today, a 2.4-meter height limit facility has been set up at both ends of the bridge, but cars and pedestrians can still pass through, allowing the ancient bridge to continue to perform its functions.

Regarding the future of Xiahuliang Bridge, Huang Zhuosheng told reporters that a few kilometers west of Xiahuliang Bridge is the origin of Zhuozhou tribute rice. According to the *Food and Money · Book of Sui*, Zhuozhou has a history of growing rice for more than 1,400 years. In 1973, when people from the United Nations Food and Agriculture Organization visited Zhuozhou, they called the area “a good place blessed with abundant resources for rice production”.

Huang Zhuosheng said: “In the future, we will build this place into a renowned rice village, which will become an ecological agricultural scenic spot. The Huliang village will be set as the drop-off place, the visitors then can walk from here to the bridge, the Huliang River, enjoy the view of rice fields, and experience the featured ecological environment, agriculture and history of Zhuozhou.”

Extended Reading: Introduction to Xiahuliang Bridge

Xiahuliang Bridge was built in the second year of Emperor Wanli in the Ming Dynasty (1574) as a single-way five-arch stone bridge. The bridge measures 69 meters long, 9.14 meters wide and 4.43 meters above the water. The railing post tops have been carved into the square shape with leave patterns. The railing posts are 1.40 meters high while the parapet panels are 0.81 meters high.

Xiahuliang Bridge and Yongji Bridge on Juma River were built in the same year. They are both important bridges in ancient capital city and have high historical, scientific and artistic values.

天水桥：见证400年城南旧事

刘靖澜 陆征 贾博钧

保定旧城南门外，一座古桥经受数百年风雨，以“南关大桥”之名为今人所熟知。今天，让我们翻开一页页旧纸，读一读它的本名和故事。

秋阳西沉，信步天水桥上。

河道两侧绿树成荫，桥下流水汩汩、波光潋滟，桥上栏杆林立、石狮各态，静静地映衬着河坡旁喧闹的集市，一动一静，仿佛浓缩了亘古久远的时光。

桥南头东侧，坐着几位耄耋老者，每日午后，他们都会来这里坐坐。虽然头上发色雪白，颊上风霜尽染，但老人们目光依然矍铄。今年已90岁高龄的曹敬先是其中最年长者。大桥附近的旧房多纳入拆迁范畴，几年前他也另觅居所，但对这片生活了几乎一辈子的地方，他仍旧难舍难离。

“老话说，过了南关桥，就是保定城。我家祖祖辈辈就住在这桥边。” 放下手中的拐杖，曹敬先缓缓抬手指向河坡东南——自己原来家的方向。“小时候，我和小伙伴们经常在河里洗澡、游泳，那时天水桥还未加宽，很窄。我年轻时是瓦匠，后来在市第二建筑公司工作，桥南边要拆的这几栋楼，当年都是我们盖的。”岁月荏苒，世事变迁，年迈的曹敬先感慨万千。

远看天水桥

天水桥，俗称“南关大桥”，位于保定市南门外府河之上。这座三孔石拱桥，桥长28米，宽7.1米，拱圈系半圆形，拱腹下净高在6米以上，是保定市现存最大的古代石桥。据《清苑县志》记载：“一亩泉自西北来，合流鸡距泉东南下，蜿蜒于城郭之南。水之上，旧有桥。兴废靡常，因革无考。”明成化二十一年（1485），改建为石桥，因一亩泉、鸡距泉出自保定西北乾位，按旧时八卦“乾”代表天，天生水，故名天水桥。该桥之后曾多次翻修翻建，现存的天水桥为明隆庆六年（1572）保定知府章时鸾兴工重建。

400余年中，经过25次特大洪峰的考验，天水桥至今仍岿然不动。其间，此处文人商贾、往来过客无数，每个晨曦初现或余晖将尽之时，人们驻足桥端，举目远眺，无不为巨桥瑰丽、天水一色的奇观而赞叹。

1952年，为使人车分流，以策安全，原桥两侧各加宽5米的人行道。1962年冬，桥面改建为预制钢筋结构，两侧木质桥栏改为金

近看天水桥

桥上石狮

属质。1984年6月，天水桥作为古建筑被列为市级文物保护单位。目前，人们所见的桥上栏板望柱是1996年保定市文物局对桥维修时的新雕之物。

研究保定历史数十年的市地方志办公室原主任尤文远，对天水桥颇有研究。他说，天水桥下的府河码头曾是保定城水路交通的枢纽。北宋淳化三年（992），便有保州知州李继宣造船百艘，运送军需民用物资。清光绪二十九年（1903），南关府河码头火车站建成，长长的铁路线从天水桥下南孔穿过。修建京汉铁路所用的物资，便是从天津港用木船运到这里，再装上火车运往工地。

20世纪30年代，天水桥开始有汽轮通津，保定地区及察南、雁北地区的土特产，由此运往天津；高阳、清苑、蠡县的土布，由此运往西北、东北及河南、江苏等地区；天津、上海、青岛及国外生产的工业品从天津运至保定，再销往土特产品生产地区，府河码头成为土特产品和工业产品的转运站与集散地。

在曹敬先关于天水桥的记忆里，最鲜明的正是那曾经的繁华："以前，这里就是保定的粮食集散地，有好几家大粮店，每天运粮的挑夫、粮商等络绎不绝。同时，这里还是运输煤炭等物资的交通枢纽。桥下是水运码头，通往白洋淀、天津卫，船家都在桥下等候坐船的乘客。河坡两旁，有许多饭馆，船家、商家的叫卖声和揽客声，到现在我都还记得。咱们保定的'址舫头''煤市街'这些地名，都跟这条河、这座桥有关。后来，河坡边又开起了打铁、锔瓷、铸锅这些行当。现如今，河坡边的这一片市场，大概是二三十年前形成的，方便附近居民购物。"

穿越数百年风雨，天水桥不仅给人们以通达便利，也见证了那段历史的繁华与精彩。中华人民共和国成立后，历尽沧桑的天水桥陪伴着一代代保定人，走过了崭新的发展历程，也期待着新时代的盛世华章。

Tianshui Bridge: Witness of the 400 Years History

Liu Jinglan Lu Zheng Jia Bojun

Outside the south gate of the old city of Baoding, an ancient bridge withstood hundreds of years of wind and rain, known by the name of "Nanguan Bridge". Today, let's turn over the old pages and read its real name and story.

The autumn sun is sinking in the west, I am strolling on the Tianshui Bridge.

With tree-lined river banks, shimmering waves under the bridge and various railings and stone lions, the silent scene around the bridge are in stark contrast to the bustling bazaar market nearby, as if the time right from the distant past had been condensed here.

On the east side of the south end of the bridge, there are several elderly people sitting here. They come here every afternoon. Although their hair on the head is snow-white and their cheeks are stained with frost, the old people's eyes are still bright. Cao Jingxian, 90 years old this year, is the oldest among them. Most of the old houses near the bridge are subject to demolition. A few years ago, he found another residence, but is still reluctant to leave this place, where he has lived for almost his entire life.

"As the old saying goes, if you cross Nanguan Bridge, you will be in Baoding. My family has lived by this bridge for generations." Laying down his crutch, Cao Jingxian slowly raised his hand and pointed to the southeast of the river slope—the direction of his original home. "When I was a little kid, my friends and I used to bathe and swim in the river. At that time, Tianshui Bridge was very narrow before it was widened. I was a bricklayer when I was young, and later I worked for the city's 2nd Construction Company. The buildings to be demolished on the south side of the bridge were all built by us back then." Things changed greatly as time flies. Cao Jingxian sighed with emotion.

Tianshui Bridge, commonly known as "Nanguan Bridge", is located on the Fuhe River outside the South Gate of Baoding city. The three-arch stone bridge, which is 28 meters long and 7.1 meters wide, has semicircular arches 6 meters above the water. It is the largest existing ancient stone bridge in Baoding City. According to the records in *Qingyuan County Annals*, "Yimu Spring comes from the northwest, and interflows with Jiju Spring toward the southeast, and runs in the south of the city. There was once a bridge above the water. It has a history of uncertainty." In 1485, the bridge was renovated into a stone bridge. According to its location in the northwest of Baoding and the philosophy of Bagua, it has been named Tianshui Bridge.

After that, Tianshui Bridge has been renovated for many times. The existing Tianshui Bridge was rebuilt by Zhang Shiluan, the prefect of Baoding in the sixth year of Emperor Longqing in the Ming Dynasty (1572).

In the past 400 years, Tianshui Bridge has survived 25 flood peaks. During those years, poets, merchants, all the visitors came and went through the bridge. At sunrise or sunset, people would stand on one side of the bridge, and look far away, impressed by the beauty of the bridge and water.

In 1952, in order to divert people and vehicles and ensure safety, the sidewalks on the original bridge were widened by 5 meters. In the winter of 1962, the bridge deck was rebuilt into a prefabricated steel structure, and the wooden bridge handrails on both sides were changed to metal. In June 1984, Tianshui Bridge, as an ancient building, was listed as a municipal cultural relics protection unit. Currently, the pillars of the bridge were new carvings renovated by the Cultural Relics Bureau in Baoding in 1996.

You Wenyuan, former director of Baoding Local Chronicle Office, who has studied the history of Baoding for decades, has done a lot of research on Tianshui Bridge. He said that the Fuhe Wharf under the Tianshui Bridge was once the hub of waterway traffic in Baoding. In the 3rd year of Emperor Chunhua in the Northern Song Dynasty (992), Li Jixuan, the governor of Baozhou, built hundreds of ships to transport military supplies and civilian materials. In the 29th year of Emperor Guangxu in the Qing Dynasty (1903), the Nanguan Fuhe Wharf Railway Station was built, and the long railway line passed through the South Hole under the Tianshui Bridge. The materials used for the construction of the Beijing-Hanzhou Railway were transported here by wooden boats from Tianjin Port, and then loaded on trains and transported to the construction site.

In the 1930s, Tianshui Bridge opened to shipping. Local products from Baoding, Chanan and Yanbei areas were transported to Tianjin; The home cloths from Gaoyang, Qingyuan and Lixian were transported to the northwest, northeast, Henan and Jiangsu provinces. Industrial products manufactured in Tianjin, Shanghai, Qingdao and abroad were transported from Tianjin to Baoding and then sold to the production areas of local special products. Fuhe Wharf has become a transfer station and distribution center of local special products and industrial products.

In Cao Jingxian's memory about Tianshui Bridge, the most striking thing is the prosperity of the past: "In the past, this was the grain distribution center of Baoding. There were several large grain stores, and an endless stream of porters and grain merchants who transported grain every day. At the same time, it was also a transportation hub for transporting coal and other materials. Under the bridge was the water transport dock leading to Baiyangdian Lake and Tianjin Wei. Boatmen were waiting there under the bridge for passengers. On both banks of the river, there were many restaurants, and I still remember the shouts from the boatmen and store owners. Some place names, such as "Zhi

桥上石狮

Fang Tou", "Mei Shi Street", are all related to this river and bridge. Since then, some businesses, including forging iron, making porcelain and casting pans emerged on both banks. Today's market was developed 20 to 30 years ago and has grown into a convenient shopping place for dwellers nearby.

After hundreds of years of wind and rain, Tianshui Bridge has not only provides people with convenient access, but also witnessed the prosperity and splendor of that period of history. After the founding of the PRC, Tianshui Bridge, which has experienced the vicissitudes of life and accompanied generations of Baoding people through a brand-new development process, is looking forward to the prosperity of the new era.

天上飞虹落莲池

赵琳 王德明

古莲花池北塘内水中有一亭，即“莲池十二景”中的宛虹亭，有“宛若天上飞虹”的意趣。亭北有曲桥，势若游龙衔接北岸；亭南有宛虹桥，如长虹凌空飞架水中。此亭巧妙地将北塘分割成东大西小两塘，每逢盛夏时节，游人居宛虹亭中，或立宛虹桥上，俯视一泓碧水，东塘红莲妩媚，西塘白莲皎洁，荷香飘逸，沁人心脾。

宛虹亭无疑是古莲花池的中心所在，如果游人只能选池中一景合影留念，势必会选此景。那么，宛虹亭究竟是何人所建？又有哪些历史故事呢？

它是临漪亭的继承者。

宛虹亭被视为元明时期临漪亭的继承者。临漪亭可追溯到元代，本为元初汝南王张柔所建“雪香园”中一景，后赐给部将乔惟忠。

1247年农历六月初一，元代学者郝经在保时，应乔惟忠次子乔德玉请求，撰写《临漪亭记》，其中写道：“出而东则亭，亭则侯之别第也。面水者三，右池而左洄，屋重而庑列，鳞渌漪然，榜曰‘临漪’。”可以看出，此亭正是乔府别墅的一部分，三面环水，右面是池塘，左面是回旋的流水，屋顶重叠而游廊布列，清澈的水流微波荡漾，所以名为临漪亭。

宛虹亭

随后，郝经又以优美的文笔写下了古莲花池曾经的盛景："茂树葱郁，异卉芬蒨，庚伏冠衣，清风戛然，迥不知暑。澄澜荡漾，帘户疏越，鱼泳而鸟翔，虽城市嚣嚣而得三湘七泽之乐，可谓胜地矣。"郝经盛赞三伏天里在池边纳凉，虽身处城市喧哗却能享受到湘楚一带湖泽风光的乐趣。

它出自直隶总督方观承。

乾隆十年（1745），古莲花池被辟为行宫。乾隆十四年（1749），直隶总督方观承对莲池行宫建筑进行大规模改建和新建。乾隆二十五年（1760），方观承将行宫景物分为十二组，命人各绘图一幅，每图系以说明。这便是"莲池十二景"的由来，而宛虹亭即为其中之一。

此亭名“宛虹”，与亭南的拱形石桥相关。方观承指出：“相如赋云：‘宛虹拖于楯轩。’缘其偃蟺水心，故取诸此。”可见，西汉司马相如的《上林赋》中有“宛虹拖于楯轩”，意为弯曲的虹越过栏杆之上。宛虹亭命名正缘于此句，因为笠亭和拱桥覆盖并相连在水塘中心。

“莲池十二景”每一景都系以方观承五古诗一首和莲池书院院长张叙七绝诗一首。

方观承的诗颇具浪漫主义色彩：“山近豁渝泉，烟波自清境。穹龟五百年，伏护一沤影。何当具扁舟，更向江湖迥。”我们似乎可以看到，方观承身着便服，漫步在古莲花池中，行至宛虹亭，将自己融入这从抱阳山而来的清泉，产生超脱人世的思想。

张叙的描写则比较具象：“天半飞虹界碧霄，一亭如笠系轻舠。浣花老叟时相过，便是西川万里桥。”感叹着，如果杜甫来这里探访，便是成都万里桥畔。

它曾被乾隆皇帝盛赞。

乾隆二十六年（1761），方观承将《莲池行宫十二景图》敬呈乾隆御览，乾隆遂于每图之后各题七绝诗一首。其中对“宛虹亭”题道：“垂虹宛宛跨堤濆，一笠横空与半分。却是清波无我见，亭桥入影惣沄沄。”垂虹指的是宛虹亭南侧的宛虹桥，此桥为单孔弧形，状若彩虹垂挂。“笠”便是笠亭，即宛虹亭。宛虹桥犹如垂虹一般，跨在池水中央，宛虹亭像一只斗笠横亘在天空，将水面平分。清澈的水波没有偏见，将亭与桥投射的倒影，都摇荡得纷乱……即便没有亲临古莲花池，读此诗也有身临其境的感觉。

它并不是最初的模样。

宛虹亭的别名有很多，如水中亭、水心亭、笠亭等。在乾隆年间莲池行宫时期，此亭是五柱圆形攒尖顶亭，形似斗笠，因此有笠亭之称。

雍正年间进士、在乾隆年间任陕西按察使的安新人陈德正就曾以《笠亭》为题，写出“天光倒影漾空明，为有源头如许清。不断生香通鼻管，泠然真作御风行”，描述了自己在亭边游览时的轻盈自在的感觉。

咸丰十一年（1861），《莲池行宫十二景图》被重新绘制，景观布局没有变化。光绪年间，宛虹亭变为八角重檐攒尖顶的双层阁亭，宛虹桥变为平式的凌空桥。

也难怪清末候补官员、重修《保定府志》的总理郭云丰，在光绪五年（1879）写下的《莲池台榭记》中有云：“由楼西南度宛虹桥，至宛虹亭，今所谓‘笠亭’，昔所谓‘临漪亭’也。亭南有‘凌空桥’，登高如在天际。”郭云丰所写的“宛虹桥”实为如今的曲步桥，而“凌空桥”则为“宛虹桥”。

它是莲池最美的景色。

1900年，八国联军侵入保定，古莲花池亭台楼阁化为灰烬。此后，直隶总督袁世凯、杨士骧等均对古莲花池进行修复，但仅藻泳楼、高芬阁、宛虹桥有所恢复。其中，宛虹桥的石拱被改为板桥。

1998年以后，保定市政府对古莲花池进行了大规模的修缮，相继修缮“莲池十二景”，宛虹亭自然也在修缮之列。我们现在所看到的宛虹亭与光绪年间的宛虹亭相同，为八角重檐攒尖顶的双层阁亭，亭有两层，高约12米，内柱之间以格扇为门窗，门内有旋转式木梯通顶层。宛虹桥为白玉石拱桥，重现长虹凌空飞架之势，令人感慨时光倏忽而过，留给后人无限思怀。

The Rainbow Crossing Lotus Pond

Zhao Lin　Wang Deming

In the north of the Ancient Lotus Pond stands a pavilion named Wanhong Pavilion, which means "a pavilion like a rainbow". It is one of the twelve scenes of Lotus Pond. In the north of the pavilion a dragon-like curved bridge connects the north bank while in the south towers Wanhong Bridge like a rainbow flying over the water. Wanhong Pavilion parts north pond into a bigger east pond and a smaller west pond. Every summer, visitors could enjoy the view of the pond in Wanhong Pavilion or on Wanhong Bridge. The red lotus in east pond is enchanting while white lotus in west pond is bright and clear, with refreshing fragrance of lotus pervading the ponds.

Wanhong Pavilion is undoubtedly the center of the Ancient Lotus Pond. If visitors can only choose one scene in the pond for a group photo, they will definitely choose this scene. So then, who built Wanhong Pavilion and what historical stories are behind it?

Wanhong Pavilion is the continuator of Linyi Pavilion.

Wanhong Pavilion is deemed to be the continuator of Linyi Pavilion that existed in the Yuan and Ming Dynasties. Linyi Pavilion can be traced back to the Yuan Dynasty. It was originally a scene in Xuexiang Garden built by Zhang Rou, the vassal king of Runan County in the early Yuan Dynasty, and was later granted to his subordinate Qiao Weizhong.

On the first day of the sixth lunar month in 1247, scholar Hao Jing of Yuan Dynasty was in Baoding. At the request of Qiao Weizhong's second son, Qiao Deyu, Hao composed *A Sketch of Linyi Pavilion*, which wrote: "A stream flows out of Qiao Weizhong's garden to the east and a pavilion stands here, in the villa of Qiao. The pavilion is surrounded by water on three sides, with a pond on the right and a swirling creek on the left. Its roof overlaps and its verandas are lined up. The clear water around the pavilion ripples softly so it is named Linyi Pavilion."

Later, Hao also wrote down the gorgeous view in the Ancient Lotus Pond, "trees are prosperous, flowers scented, and the breeze blowing, far from heat. Water flows, curtain waves, fish swim and birds fly up high. It is a perfect place to hide away from the noise in town." To sum up, Hao highly praised the fine view of Ancient Lotus Pond in this sketch.

Wanhong Pavilion was named by Fang Guancheng, the governor of Zhili Province.

In the 10th year of Emperor Qianlong of Qing Dynasty (1745), the Ancient Lotus Pond was developed into a palace. In the 14th year of Emperor Qianlong (1749), Fang Guancheng rebuilt and constructed the buildings of the Lotus Pond Palace on a large scale. In the 25th year of Emperor Qianlong (1760), he divided the palace scenery into twelve groups, and had an illustrative picture drawn for each scenery. This is the origin of the "Twelve Scenes of Lotus Pond", and Wanhong Pavilion is one of them.

The name "Wanhong" is related to the arched stone bridge in the south of the pavilion. Fang Guancheng also pointed out, "In *Odes by Xiangru*, it said, 'it is like rainbow sitting on the door and rails'. As it is sitting in the water, it is so named." The name "Wanhong Pavilion" comes exactly from this ode since the pavilion and the arched bridge were linked and they covered the center of the pond.

Fang Guancheng composed a five-character poem for each scene of Twelve Scenes of Lotus Pond while Zhang Xu, the dean of Lotus Pond Academy wrote a seven-character quatrain for each of them.

Fang Guancheng's poem is rather romantic, "Yushui River suddenly runs underground close to Baoyang Mountain, to become a spring; the misty water in the Lotus Pond comes from the tranquil mysterious place at the foot of Baoyang Mountain. Baoyang Mountain has been lying on its stomach and protecting the mirror-like pond for five hundred years. Nature is so profound and subtle that it is hard to understand. I wonder when I can prepare a boat and row it towards my remote hometown dotted with rivers and lakes." It seems right in front of our eyes that Fang Guancheng casually dressed wandered around the Lotus Pond, and fused himself into the clear spring from Baoyang Mountain at the Wanhong Pavilion, when he had the idea of detachment from the secular world.

A painting seemed to be portrayed in this poem that Fang Guancheng, in his informal dress roamed in Ancient Lotus Pond and when he walked to Wanhong Pavilion, he integrated himself into the clear spring from Baoyang Mountain and his thought detached from the earthliness.

Zhang Xu gave a specific description, "The tall arch bridge divides the sky into two halves in midair; beside a pavilion with a roof like a bamboo hat, a swift boat is anchored. If Du Fu sees me often in the Lotus Pond Academy, here can be compared to the side of the Wanli Bridge in Chengdu, where Du Fu's thatched cottage is located." He gave the exclamation that here would be the bank of Wanli Bridge if Du Fu visited him here.

Wanhong Pavilion was once highly praised by Emperor Qianlong.

In 1761, Fang submitted the "Twelve scenes of the Lotus Pond" to Qianlong, and the Emperor wrote four-line poems for each scene. He wrote about "Wan Hong Pavilion", "The bridge is like a rainbow connecting the banks, the Pavilion divides the water into two halves. The clean water ripples, reflecting the bridge and Pavilion". The "bridge" refers to the Rainbow Bridge in the south, an arc-shaped bridge looking like a rainbow. The "Pavilion" is the "Wan Hong Pavilion". The poem means that the bridge is like a rainbow across the pond, and the Pavilion is like a hat hung in the middle, dividing the water. The clear water is not biased and, rippling and reflecting both the

宛虹亭

Pavilion and bridge. Even we are not there, through these lines, we can picture and feel the breathtaking scenery.

Wanhong Pavilion was not the original look afterwards.

Wanhong Pavilion has many other names such as Shuizhong Pavilion (the pavilion in the water), Shuixin Pavilion (the pavilion in the center of water) and Li Pavilion (the pavilion like a bamboo hat). During the reign of Emperor Qianlong, it was a five-column circular pavilion with a pointed roof, which look like a bamboo hat, so it was also called Li Pavilion then.

Chen Dezheng from Anxin, who was a Jinshi (metropolitan graduate) and acted as surveillance commissioner of Shaanxi during Emperor Qianlong's reign, once wrote a poem titled Li Pavilion, "The bright sky is reflected clearly in the rippling water, which comes from a crystal clear source. Smelling continuous fragrance, I seem to be really riding the cool breeze." The poem shows that he felt relaxed and comfortable during sightseeing beside the pavilion.

In the 11th year of Emperor Xianfeng of Qing Dynasty (1861), Twelve Scenes of Lotus Pond Palace was redrawn with the landscape layout unchanged. In the years of Emperor Guangxu, Wanhong Pavilion was reshaped to double-layer pavilion with octagonal double eaves and spires and Wanhong Bridge was reconstructed to a flat overhead bridge.

It is no wonder that Guo Yunfeng, a candidate official in the late Qing dynasty and the leader of recompiling the *Annals of Baoding City*, wrote in his *Records of Platforms and Pavilions on the Lotus Pond*, "Across Wanhong Bridge from the southwest of the tower, we arrive at Wanhong Pavilion, known as 'Li Pavilion' now but 'Linyi Pavilion' before. To the south of the pavilion, there is the 'Lingkong Bridge', on the top of which it seems as if we were in the sky." The "Wanhong Bridge" recorded by Guo Yunfeng is actually the current Qubu Bridge, while "Lingkong Bridge" is "Wanhong Bridge".

Wanhong Pavilion is the most beautiful view of the Lotus Pond.

In 1900, the Eight-Power Allied Forces invaded Baoding, and the pavilions, terraces and towers of Ancient Lotus Pond were destroyed to ashes. After that, the governor of Zhili Province Yuan Shikai and his successor Yang Shixiang have renovated Ancient Lotus Pond, but only Zaoyong Tower, Gaofen Tower and Wanhong Bridge were partly restored. Among them, the arched Wanhong Bridge were transformed into a slab bridge.

After 1998, Baoding Municipal government carried out large-scale repairs to the Ancient Lotus Pond including Wanhong Pavilion. All of the twelve scenes of Lotus Pond including Wanhong Pavilion were restored. Wanhong Pavilion we could see today is the same with the one during the reign of Emperor Guangxu, a double-layer pavilion with octagonal double eaves and spires. The pavilion is twelve meters high with wooden partitions between its inner columns as doors and windows. And there is a revolving wooden ladder inside the door to the top floor. Wanhong Bridge now is a arch marble bridge, reproducing the image of aloft rainbow, which arouses the sighs of fleeting time and leaves infinite thoughts to future generations.

铜帮铁底金线河

——兼谈『太平桥』的文物内涵

王锡峰

清苑中冉村北，潺潺流水的金线河，业已断流60年。昔日，一群光腚顽童相拥着从石桥上跳入河中顺流戏水，惊得那三五成群的黄姑鱼儿纷纷跃出水面察看，吓得那远处的几只水鸡急忙潜入水底，连那倒映在水中的两岸堤坝和歪脖柳树也被搅得一塌糊涂。那些戴草帽拿锄头种田的农民、背渔网赤双足捕鱼的渔夫、南来北往进城下乡的客商，每天在石桥上穿梭而行，络绎不绝。

如今，这条43公里长的金线河，绝大部分已变成良田。只有那座万历年间重修的古石桥，依然孤寂歪斜地静卧在故河道上，不厌其烦地向过往路人诉说着往昔的沧桑。

太行北端，有一座挺拔秀丽、直刺云天的狼牙山。从狼牙山沿着山深林密、峰峦峻峭的太行山脉南行，很快便进入今天的顺平县境。

顺平，史称曲逆国，亦称蒲阴国。蒲阴东南，有一条五狼沟，和太行山脉相连。沟内巨岩层现，涧曲泉清。在那蜿蜒起伏的山涧里，泉水从各个狭小而深邃的山石间不断地往外喷涌。一股股涓涓细流从山谷中不停地转出，越聚越多、越流越湍、越湍越急，撞到山根的石头上，立刻像千千万万的珍珠四处散花。忽然，一块貌似巨鱼的大石，拦腰挡住了河水的去路，逼着河水不得不“曲而西流”。这就是郦道元在《水经注》中提到的曲逆河啊!

史称其 “枉渚回湍，率多曲复，亦谓之为曲逆水也” 。后因曲逆不善，改称蒲阴河。

曲逆河也好，蒲阴河也罢，它一头向西南逆行，经过千回百转，拐来拐去，最后还是乖乖地向东南方向流去。在方顺桥村西，汇流泻入金线河和百草沟。

据《清苑县志》顺治十七年（1660）所载，（金线）河之上流有二，一自满城之方顺河，一自庆都之龙泉河，至魏村两水汇为一，东流至此（中冉、北大冉）成巨津也。

金线河流经清苑的魏村、白团、中冉、北大冉、赵庄、石桥等村，从莲花闸注入府河，与漕河汇流后，通过白洋淀入海。金线河河道弯曲，穿村较多。

金线河，是一条历史悠久的河流，源于蒲阴。随着高山平湖、沧海桑田的剧烈变迁，明朝嘉靖年间的《清苑县志》记载，金线河已成为旱则干枯、雨则泛涨、汛则漫溢的季节性河流，一遇暴雨，漫溢成灾。

金线河，仅据1954—1964年统计，就有7年漫溢决口，造成不同程度的损失。1963年，遭遇百年不遇的特大洪灾后，随着清水河、龙泉河的治理，京广铁路以西的所有水源被导入龙泉河，金线河成为无源之水，旧河道慢慢被填平。

金线河，是一条美丽的河流，从中冉村北边缓缓流过。说它美丽，一是因其风景秀丽，景色迷人；二是因其有很多美丽的传说和趣闻。

金线河，河床不宽，河道不深，堤坝也不高，河水时有时无，时高时低，却被三里五乡的百姓们誉为“铜帮铁底”金线河。

笔者小时候，听村里的老人们念叨，金线河是后周末年，宋太祖赵匡胤在清苑故居招兵买马时，开凿的一条运粮河。最早修建的“太平桥”，大约建于1000多年前的宋太宗登基后的太平兴国年间。

金线河弯弯曲曲的两道长堤，都是由清一色的黄土堆成，在阳光照射下像金子一样闪闪发光；而河底却是坚硬的黑泥，像铁一样乌黑，它湿了黏，干了硬，不湿不干刨不动。

在金线河的河床上，盘根错节地生长着两种野草：一种叫铜网根，因根茎被淡红色的薄皮包裹而得名；一种叫铁网根，因根茎被浅黑色的薄皮包裹而得名。它们的根茎十分发达，穿透力极强，有的可达丈余，凡是有根茎的地方，就能从节间发芽生长，繁殖能力极强。

这两种野草，无花无果，叶子又长又窄又尖，既耐旱又耐涝。大旱3年，其依然存活，任凭洪水冲刷，风吹雨打，仍然牢牢地钉在河床上，年复一年地保护着金线河。老人们说的铜帮铁底金线河，其实是因这两种野草而得名的。

“铜帮铁底金线河，三条腿的蛤蟆多。”这是金线河的又一奇观。从小（石）桥顺着河堤向东北方向的北大冉村走，大约500米左右，有一片榆树坟。在这段金线河边，不知什么原因，经常有一些畸形的三条腿的蛤蟆出没，而在全村别的地方，却一只也没有。

人们常说，两条腿的人到处都是，三条腿的蛤蟆无处找寻。而在这段金线河边，你可以经常看见三条腿的蛤蟆到处跳跃。

中冉村北的金线河上，有两座古石桥，距古城保定，不足10公里之遥。

西边的“太平桥”，俗称大（石）桥。此桥南北走向，宽5

米，长16米，桥下有8排散柱，桥面有7列条石，南北引桥各5米，是魏村、冉庄一带老百姓进城购物、保定商人贩货下乡的必经之路，曾是一条繁忙的运输通道。

东边的“通天桥”比较窄，桥面也是条石结构，桥桩由几排圆柱石墩堆砌而成，人们习惯叫它小（石）桥。此桥主要为方便种地所修。它是安国、博野、蠡县一带农民进城的要道之一。

两座古石桥，由何人于何时建成，因年代久远，已无据可考。如今只有太平桥下的横梁上“万历四十一年孟春重修”几个字，仍然清晰可见。古石桥的历史可见一斑，古石桥最晚建造也应是在400多年前的明朝。

古石桥，它见证了清朝最后一名状元刘春霖赶着三套马车到中冉岳丈家吊孝拜灵的场景；古石桥，它是爱国将领冯玉祥经常到中冉摔跤会友的必经之路；古石桥，它还是中冉村老党员郭大义拉洋车时和地下党的城工部秘密传递情报的联络点。古石桥特别值得一提的是，1963年特大洪水到来的前一天，中冉村参加过“群英会”的全国劳模郭淑芳大娘，曾在四个青年的护送下，冒雨从桥上蹚着齐腰深的河水，到南沟头村接生救人。

现在，小（石）桥已被挖沙土坑的人所毁，桥面丢失，桥墩难觅，历史影像已消失得无影无踪。大（石）桥也早已荒废多年，如不及早采取措施进行修复保护，过不了多久，恐怕也将荡然无存。

笔者小时候，每逢夏日都能看到浑黄的金线河水潺潺东流。河两侧那弯弯的长堤，坡上坡下，绿草如茵。红、白、黄、蓝、紫等各色野花点缀其中，红的似火，白的如玉，黄的呈金，蓝的像宝石，紫的赛翡翠，真可谓姹紫嫣红，绚丽多姿，五彩缤纷，美不胜收。小桥北岸，紧靠堤坡有一眼水井，八卦水车旁的两棵刺槐，高大挺拔，枝繁叶茂，荫蔽数丈。串串槐花，迎风摇曳，散发着迷人的馨香。蝴蝶在百花间漫舞，蚂蚱在草丛中爬行，喜鹊在河面上嬉耍，小鸟在树冠中高鸣。从远处看去，犹如一幅美丽的图画。

那蜿蜒东去的金线河水，无私地滋润着两岸河床上的大豆和高粱。那些枝枝杆杆蔓蔓叶叶，严严实实盖满河床，微风吹起，红绿掩映，累累果实，随风摆动，堤内堤外，一派丰收景象。

如今，这美丽的铜帮铁底金线河，只留下美好的记忆。

据介绍，清苑区委、区政府对这座古石桥非常重视，已于2015年将之定为县级文物。村民们保护文物的意识也日益增强，自发地组成了护桥队。大家期盼金线河上仅有的历史文物，尽快被修复和保护起来，传承并发扬光大，给子孙后代留下一些怀念历史的寄托。

Jinxian River and the Cultural Implications of Taiping Bridge

Wang Xifeng

To the north of Zhongran Village in Qingyuan, the gurgling Jinxian River has been dry for 60 years. In the past, a bunch of naked children would joyfully dive from the stone bridge into this river to play, which startled schools of fish to jump out and water hens hastily hide beneath the water, as well as disrupted the perfect reflections of embankments and crooked-neck willows. Peasants wearing straw hats and carrying hoes, fishermen walking barefoot and merchants traveling back and forth between urban and rural areas pass through the stone bridge every day.

Today, most of the 43-kilometer-long Jinxian River has become fertile land. Only the ancient stone bridge, which was rebuilt during the Wanli period, still lies lonely and crooked on the old river, tirelessly telling passers-by about the vicissitudes of the past.

In the north of the Taihang mountains is the stiff, sky-soaring Langya Mountain. Running southwards along Taihang Mountains deeming with dense forests and towering peaks, the Langya Mountain has an impressive presence in Shunping County.

Shunping, known as Quni state in history, is also named Puyin state. In the southeast of Puyin, there is Wulanggou Ditch, which is connected with Taihang Mountains. Layers of giant rocks and clear streams can be found in the mountain's gully. Along the zigzag mountain streams, springs pop out constantly from various narrow, deep rock gaps. Trickles of spring water constantly flow out of the mountain valley and then they converge into torrential flows. When they crash on the rocks at the foot of the mountain, there will be millions of water drops bursting out like pearls. Abruptly, a giant fish-shaped rock blocks the river flow, forcing it to "make a westward turn". This is Quni River mentioned by Li Daoyuan in his *Commentary on the Water Classic*!

In historic records, "The river curves along the land with whirly torrents, and is also known as Quni River given its many turns". Later, it was renamed Puyin River due to infelicitous implications of the name.

Whether it is called Quni River or Puyin River, it eventually flows to the southeast despite thousands of its turns and reverse flows. The river converges into the Jinxian River and Baicao Gully in the west of Fangshun Bridge Village.

According to records of the *Annals of Qingyuan County*, in the 17th year of Emperor Shunzhi's reign (1660), there were two upper streams of Jinxian River: the first was the Fangshun River of Mancheng and the second was the Longquan River of Qingdu. The two rivers joined at Wei Village and flowed eastward to become a large-sized river here (Zhongran, Beidaran).

Jinxian River flows through Weicun, Baituan, Zhongran, Beidaran, Zhaozhuang, Shiqiao and other villages in Qingyuan. It enters Fuhe River from Lianhua Gate and merges with Caohe River before entering the sea through Baiyangdian Lake. Jinxian River has a curved channel and passes through many villages.

Jinxian River is a river with a long history, originating from Puyin. With the dramatic changes in the mountains and lakes and the vicissitudes of life, the *Qingyuan County Chronicle* in the Jiajing period of the Ming Dynasty recorded that Jinxian River has become a seasonal river that dries up in drought, swells in rain and overflows in flood. When it rains, the river overflows, causing severe disasters.

According to the statistics from 1954 to 1964, Jinxian River overflowed and burst in 7 years, causing different degrees of losses. In 1963, after encountering a catastrophic flood that was rare in a century, with the management of Qingshui River and Longquan River, all the water sources west of the Beijing-Guangzhou Railway were channeled into Longquan River, Jinxian River became a sourceless water, and the old river was slowly filled up.

Jinxian River, a beautiful river, flows slowly in the north of Zhongran village. Its beauty comes from two sources: first, beautiful natural scenes; second, beautiful stories and anecdotes.

Jinxian River does not have a wide riverbed, deep channel or high dykes. The water flow of the river changes from time to time: sometimes it dries up and other times it floods. Therefore, the river is acclaimed by locals as Jinxian River with "copper embankments and iron bottom".

When I was a child, I heard the old people in the village say that Jinxian River was dug for transporting grain by Zhao Kuangyin, the emperor Taizu of the Song Dynasty, when he was recruiting troops and horses at his former residence in Qingyuan. Taiping Bridge is the earliest bridge on the river built in the Taiping Xingguo period, about 1, 000 years ago after Emperor Taizong of Song took the throne.

The winding dikes of Jinxian River are built with loess which glitters like gold under the sun; while the bottom of the river is solid black mud - like iron, which turns sticky in wet conditions, solidifies in dry conditions and is difficult to excavate when it is neither too wet or too dry.

On the riverbed of Jinxian river are two varieties of weeds that entangle with each other: one is called the "Copper Net Roots" because its rhizome is covered by a thin light red layer; the other is called "Iron Net Roots" because its rhizome is covered by a thin black layer. Their rhizomes are strong, highly penetrative and can grow up to 12 feet. Wherever they are, these rhizomes are able to sprout and reproduce vigorously.

These two kinds of weeds have no flowers or fruits, and their leaves are long, narrow and sharp. They are both resistant to drought and flood. After 3 years of drought, it still survived; Despite the flood, wind and rain, it is still firmly nailed to the riverbed and protects Jinxian River year after year. "copper embankments and iron bottom" mentioned by the old people is actually named after these two kinds of weeds.

"There are many three-legged toads in Jinxian River with copper embankments and iron bottom". This is another wonder of Jinxian River. The small (stone) bridge goes along the river bank to Beidaran Village in the northeast. About 500 meters away, there is an Elm Grave. In this section of Jinxian River, for some reason, there are often some deformed three-legged toads, but there are none in the other parts of the village.

It is often said that two-legged people are everywhere, and three-legged toads are nowhere to be found. In this section of Jinxian River, you can often see three-legged toads jumping around.

On Jinxian River in the north of Zhongran Village, there are two ancient stone bridges, less than 10 kilometers away from the ancient city of Baoding.

"Taiping Bridge" in the west is commonly known as the big (stone) bridge. The bridge runs north-south, with a width of 5 meters and a length of 16 meters. There are 8 rows of scattered columns under the bridge, 7 rows of stones on the bridge deck and 5-meter-long North and South approach bridge. It is the only way for people in Weicun and Ranzhuang to go shopping in the city and for Baoding businessmen to sell goods to the countryside. It was once a busy transportation channel.

"Tongtian Bridge" in the East is relatively narrow, and the bridge deck is also a strip stone structure. The bridge piles are stacked by several rows of cylindrical stone piers. People are used to calling it a small (stone) bridge, which is mainly built for the convenience of planting land. It is one of the main roads for farmers in Anguo, Boye and Lixian to get to town.

There are no historical records about who built the two ancient stone bridges and when they were built. Today, on the beam under Taiping Bridge, the words "Reconstructed by Mengchun in the 41st year of Emperor Wanli" are still clearly visible, which reveals the history of the ancient stone bridge.

The latest construction of the ancient stone bridge should have been in the Ming Dynasty more than 400 years ago.

The ancient stone bridge has witnessed the last zhuangyuan (who was ranked first-class in the palace examination) Liu Chunlin rode a three-horse wagon to attend the funeral of his father-in-law in Zhongran; it was also the place where the patriotic general Feng Yuxiang frequently passed by to meet his wrestling friends in Zhongran; it was also the contact point where party member Guo Dayi from Zhongran Village secretly exchanged intelligence with underground City Work Department. It is particularly worth mentioning that the day before the onset of the huge flood in 1963, Guo Shufang, a national model worker from Zhongran Village who was honored to attend the "Outstanding Workers Conference", was escorted by four young lads in heavy rain, crossing the waist-deep water to help deliver a baby at Nangoutou Village.

Now, the small (stone) bridge has been destroyed by people digging sand pits, the bridge deck is lost, the piers are hard to find, and the historical image has disappeared without a trace. The large (stone) bridge has long been abandoned for many years. If measures are not taken to repair and protect it as soon as possible, it will not be long before it disappears.

When I was a child, I could see the muddy yellow Jinxian River flowing eastward every summer. The long winding banks on both sides of the river are covered with green grass. Red, white, yellow, blue, purple and other colors of wild flowers are dotted among them. The red is like fire, the white is like jade, the yellow is like gold, the blue is like a gem, and the purple is like emerald. A great variety of splendidly colorful wild flowers are also quite a scene.

On the bank north of the small bridge, there is a well adjacent to the embankment, beside the Bagua waterwheel of which are two tall straight locust trees with luxuriant foliage, stretching to shade a large area. Strings of sophora flowers swing in the breeze and give off charming fragrance. Butterflies flutter their wings through a great variety of flowers; locusts crawl through meadows; magpies are frolicking on the river; birds are singing sonorously in canopies. It looks like a beautiful painting in the distance.

Jinxian River, which winds eastward, selflessly nourishes the soybeans and sorghum on both sides of the riverbed. When the breeze blows, colorful flows and countless fruits wave in the wind, presenting a picture of harvest across the dikes.

Now, this beautiful Jinxian River leaves only beautiful memories.

According to reports, Qingyuan District Party Committee and District Government attach great importance to this ancient stone bridge and have designated it as a county-level cultural relic in 2015. The villagers' awareness of protecting cultural relics is also increasing, and they spontaneously formed a bridge protection team. All locals anxiously expect that the only historic structure along Jinxian River could be repaired and protected soon so that we can preserve some of the historic memories for our descendants.

绿野梯桥：800年古韵流芳

任奕葳

冬日的古莲花池内游客并不多。走在这座由元代汝南王张柔所建的具有几百年历史的园林中，仿佛在踏着历史的脚步前行。南行，一座并不起眼的小桥，却已在此矗立了近800年，这就是古莲花池内现存最古老的建筑——绿野梯桥。瑟瑟寒风卷起枯叶，飘到桥上，盘旋而又落于水面，为这座古桥平添了几分历史的厚重感。

据莲池书院博物馆接待科科长刘丹介绍，1227年，元汝南王张柔初建园林时，就有了这座小桥。现在桥身上的每一块白玉石板都是大约800年前的，可以说这座桥见证了古莲花池大约800年的历史。

“你们看，桥栏杆很多部位都呈颗粒状风化状态，专家鉴定，这些白玉石是元代的。栏杆上的净瓶莲叶透雕，是中华人民共和国成立后修葺时新装饰的。”刘丹指着桥身说。

随后，她又着重介绍了桥拱上的兽头装饰：“这个就是老百姓口中所说的吞水兽，传说可以作镇水之用。每个年代的雕刻艺术都是不一样的，你们看这兽头雕刻表现了粗犷而古朴的特色，这是典型的元代风格。”

在河北农业大学附近居住的周芳女士每天都要来古莲花池遛弯健身。“我喜欢这里的环境，每天来这里心情都很好。”对于绿野梯桥

大雪覆盖绿野梯桥

约800年的历史，周女士惊奇地表示，“元代的文物，能保存这么好，这真是咱们保定的骄傲！”

刘丹说：“1289年，保定曾发生过一次7级左右的大地震，园中其他建筑基本被震毁，只有这座小桥完好无损，而且园中的荷花一年比一年开得好，历久不衰，百姓口中莲花池的叫法就是这么来的。”1900年，八国联军侵入保定后，在古莲花池内放火，主要建筑被焚毁殆尽，3万余册藏书被毁，珍贵文物也被洗劫一空，整个园子只留下绿野梯桥。因为小桥是石质的，又是横跨于水面之上，所以幸免于难。

由于历史悠久，桥身出现多处风化的迹象，出于安全因素的考虑，目前绿野梯桥是封闭的，没有对游客开放。刘丹说：“节假日客流量剧增，小桥的栏杆并不高，出于安全因素和对文物的保护考虑，我们于2017年把绿野梯桥封闭了，游客不能从上面走过，只能

对绿野梯桥进行保护

远看。但是绿野梯桥是我们讲解的重点内容，所以游客来到这里都会了解到它的悠久历史。”

小桥流水，风吹涟漪。尽管天气寒冷，却丝毫不影响园中的美景。只见不时有拿着相机的游客路过，到绿野梯桥附近取景拍照。

乾隆二十五年（1760），直隶总督方观承将园中景物分为十二组，各绘一图，皆有说明和题诗。他在描述寒绿轩时写道：“竹径斜出，萦带清流，石桥亘其上，修整莹洁，曰‘绿野梯桥’。”刘丹说，这仿佛勾勒出一幅水墨画卷，竹林中有条小路倾斜地延伸出来，围绕着清澈的水流，一座石桥横跨在水流上面，秀美端庄，晶莹洁白，叫作“绿野梯桥”。这不仅写明了桥的位置，而且对桥的外观与质地也有所描写。

“为了维护古莲花池内所有的建筑，每年都有专家来进行鉴定。绿野梯桥是我们维护的重点，每年都要对其做加固维修工作。”刘丹说。

刘丹告诉记者，园中还有一座宛虹桥，始建于清乾隆年间，主体为木质结构，后被大火焚毁，1975年重建成单孔的汉白玉石桥。顾名思义，这座桥像彩虹卧于水上，亭台楼阁，十分美丽，是古莲花池内的必游之地，只是不如绿野梯桥的历史那么悠久。

67岁的张冬老先生家住复兴路，带着相机在古莲花池内流连许久，他说：“今天没事想起到古莲花池看看，夏天的时候来过，想看看冬天又有什么变化。”

延伸阅读：绿野梯桥简介

绿野梯桥位于篇留洞西南，是三拱梯形桥，建于元代，是古莲花池内现存最古老的建筑。该桥跨于南塘之东沟上，呈南北走向，长9.65米，宽2.65米，最大跨径2米。桥身通体用汉白玉砌成，修整莹洁，下有三拱。主拱上的吞水兽造型古朴浑厚，刀法粗犷洗练，具有典型的元代风格，与赵州桥有异曲同工之妙。栏杆上的净瓶莲叶透雕是中华人民共和国成立后修葺时新装饰的。桥名取自唐代著名宰相裴度的私家园林，据《唐书·裴度传》记载，裴度晚年在洛阳午桥建的别墅叫“绿野堂”，在洛阳集贤里府邸园林中有“梯桥”，故而此桥命名为“绿野梯桥”。

Green Field Stairway Bridge: 800 Years of Ancient Charm

Ren Yiwei

There are not many tourists in the Ancient Lotus Pond in winter. Wandering in this garden with hundreds of years' history built by Runan Lord, Zhang Rou in the Yuan Dynasty, we seem to walk into the history.

Southbound, a humble bridge has been standing here for nearly 800 years. This is the oldest existing building in the Ancient Lotus Pond — Green Field Stairway Bridge. Dead leaves picked up by cold winds drift onto the bridge, swirl and fall back onto the water, giving the old bridge a sense of history.

According to Liu Dan, head of the reception section of the Lotus Pond Academy Museum, the bridge was built in 1227 when Zhang Rou, Runan Lord in the Yuan Dynasty, built the garden. Each white jade slab on the bridge is about 800 years old. It can be said that the bridge has witnessed the history of the Ancient Lotus Pond for about 800 years.

"As you can see, there are many parts in the handrails of the bridge weathered, and it has been proofed by experts that these white marble stones were from the Yuan Dynasty. While the carvings of vase and lotus in the handrail were decorated after the founding of New China." Liu Dan pointed to the bridge and said.

Later, she introduced the decoration of the beast head on the bridge arch: "this is what people call the water beast. It is said that it can be used to hold water. The carving art of each era is different. You see, this animal head carving shows ruggedness and simplicity, which is a typical style of the Yuan Dynasty."

Ms. Zhou Fang, who lives near Hebei Agricultural University, comes to the Ancient Lotus Pond for a walk every day. "I like the environment here. I feel enjoyable when I come here every day." For the nearly 800. year history of Green Field Stairway Bridge, Ms. Zhou said in surprise, "it is the pride of Baoding that the cultural relics of the Yuan Dynasty can be preserved so well!"

Liu Dan said: "in 1289 A.D., there was a major earthquake with a magnitude of about 7 in Baoding, and other buildings in the park were destroyed by the earthquake. Only this small bridge was intact, and the lotus flowers in the park grew year by year for a long time. That's how the Lotus Pond got its name." In 1900, after the Eight Power Allied Forces invaded Baoding, they set fire to the Ancient Lotus Pond. The main buildings were burned down, more than 30,000 books were destroyed, and precious cultural relics were looted. Green Field Stairway Bridge was the only building left in the garden. The bridge survived because it was made of stone and straddled the water.

Due to its long history, there are many signs of weathering on the bridge. Green Field Stairway Bridge is currently closed to visitors for safety reasons. Liu Dan said: "A stream of visitors surged in holidays, but the handrail is not high enough, thus we closed the bridge out of safety and historic preservation purposes in 2017. Visitors can not pass the bridge and have to view the bridge in distance. However, this Green Field Stairway Bridge is our main attraction. Visitors would come here to learn about its long history."

As a small bridge over the flowing stream rippling in the wind, it provides a pastoral scene despite the cold weather. From time to time, tourists with cameras pass by and take pictures near Green Field Stairway Bridge.

In the 25th year of Emperor Qianlong (1760), the governor of Zhili Province, the local governor Fang Guancheng divided the garden into 12 groups, each presenting a picture with illustrations and poems. He described Han Lv Pavilion as "Bamboos came outside, streams run through, and a stone

绿野梯桥

桥拱上的兽头

bridge is above, white and clean. Thus, it is called the Green Field Stairway Bridge." Ms. Liu said, "it seems like a scroll of ink painting. A path stretches out of the bamboo forest around the clear water, and a stone bridge spans the water, beautiful and dignified. It's called the Green Field Stairway Bridge. This not only indicates the location of the bridge, but also describes its appearance and texture. "

"To preserve all architectural structures within the Ancient Lotus Pond, we invited experts on a yearly basis to conduct evaluations on them. Green Field Stairway Bridge is the focus of our maintenance, and we need to reinforce and repair it every year." Liu said.

Liu told reporters that there is also a Wanhong Bridge in the park, which was built during the reign of Emperor Qianlong of the Qing Dynasty. The main body of it is a wooden structure, which was burned down by a fire. The single-hole white marble bridge was rebuilt in 1975. Like its name, this bridge is like a rainbow above the water. Together with the pavilion, it creates a beautiful and harmonious view. This is a must-go place in this Lotus Pond, but not as ancient as the Green Field Stairway Bridge.

Mr. Zhang Dong, 67 years old, who lives in Fuxing Road, lingered in the Ancient Lotus Pond with his camera for a long time. He said, "since I am quite idle today, I decided to visit this place. I once visited here in summer and wondered what has changed in winter. "

Extended Reading: Introduction to Green Field Stairway Bridge

Green Field Stairway Bridge is located in the southwest of Pianliudong. It is a three-arch trapezoidal bridge. Built in the Yuan Dynasty, it is the oldest existing building in the Ancient Lotus Pond. The bridge spans over the Donggou of Nantang and runs north-south. It is 9.65 meters long, 2.65 meters wide and has a maximum span of 2 meters. The entire bridge is built with clean and neat white marble with three arches under it. The statues of the water beast in the main arch look simple and solid, the carvings are rough, which is the typical Yuan style, and similar to the Zhaozhou bridge. The carvings of vase and lotus in the handrail were decorated after the founding of New China. Its name originated from the private garden of Pei Du, a famous prime minister in the Tang Dynasty. According to records of *Pei Du Biography of the Book of Tang*, Pei Du had a villa named "Green Field Hall" in Wuqiao, Luoyang City during his late years; there was also a "stairway bridge" in the garden of his Jixianli House in Luoyang. Therefore, the bridge is named "Green Field Stairway Bridge".

莲池秀障春午坡

赵琳 王德明

初冬时节，步入古莲花池，迎面而来的假山枝蔓像一架秀美屏风，这便是“莲池十二景”之一，被称作“蓬莱仙境第一山”的春午坡。

清乾隆十年（1745），古莲花池被辟为行宫。自乾隆十四年（1749）开始，在直隶总督方观承的主持修建下，园林的亭台楼阁焕然一新，乾隆在乾隆四十六年（1781）写诗回忆时曾说：“亭台增新样，端乃开于方。”说的就是这段往事。乾隆二十五年（1760），方观承将莲池景物分组，绘图十二幅。虽然“莲池十二景”排名不分先后，但人们总会不自觉地将“春午坡”视为第一景，或许由于步入古莲花池时，首先映入眼帘的便是它。

乾隆二十六年（1761），乾隆第三次西巡五台山归来，驻跸保定，方观承将托裱好的十二幅莲池景图悉数呈乾隆御览。在方观承亲自撰写的十二景图说明文字中，我们可以寻到有关春午坡的记载：

> 春午坡，入门秀障也。锦亭斜透，修廊翼然，叠石透迁，坡陀掩映。高下杂植牡丹数百本，每春日花开，暖香延袖，真如坡诗所谓“午景发浓艳，一笑当及时”也。循廊左，别出小院，植立丰碑二，有亭覆之，曰“明职亭”。中刻明吕新吾先生训守令语，休宁太宰汪文端公谨堂书

春午坡一景

之。坡前，循廊右出，为濯锦亭，抵池北岸。

从文中可知，春午坡下种着数百株牡丹，春暖花开时带有温暖气息的香味。北宋文学家苏东坡在《雨中看牡丹三首（其二）》中写道：“明日雨当止，晨光在松枝。清寒入花骨，肃肃初自持。午景发浓艳，一笑当及时。依然暮还敛，亦自惜幽姿。”“午景发浓艳”五个字总结了观赏牡丹的最佳时期，“春午坡”景名即取意于此。

据了解，曾经的古莲花池主门左右有旁门，进入主门是一座四面由院墙封闭，供停放车、轿的小庭院，进入二门就是春午坡，其当园林之大门而立，所以方观承形容其为“入门秀障”。

其实，关于春午坡的造林艺术，我们还能从文字中读出更多的深意，同时结合相关史料记载，勾勒出一幅完美的春景图。

春午坡景是以对山为中心，四面由院墙、游廊相隔组成南北长约百米、东西宽约数十米的方形空间。对山和东、北、西三面

春午坡

院墙之间，有狭窄的曲径可绕山而行，呈东南走向，所以说“叠石逶迁”。东南近处还有一座小假山，时隐时现。秀美的亭子在偏斜的方向上通透无遮挡，此亭为明职亭，亭内有明代抚臣吕坤训守令碑。

向西穿过庭院可与万卷楼相通，西南则是濯锦亭居中的环廊，长廊开张之状，像鸟展翅欲飞的样子。循游廊入内园，顿时豁然开朗，绿荷碧水，亭台楼阁，花木掩映，先山后水，犹如置身山水画中。

春午坡借花木抒发情愫，在景观上自然颇有一番讲究。春午坡原有假山两座，中间有一土坡相连，坡上遍植芍药、牡丹。清代名士对此景作诗抒情者众多，直隶总督方观承有诗云：“林风散朝步，岩径意所适。岩畔罗春花，晴光艳如织。佳赏贵及时，何为香偶即。”莲池书院院长张叙也曾写道：“石径坡陀路几重，到门何处觅云踪。花光泼眼春当午，引入蓬莱第一峰。”

远观春午坡

清同治年间，春午坡景观未有显著变化。清光绪年间，春午坡仍在，在郭云丰的《莲池台榭记》中记载："池门北向，内为重门。屏于重门者，为春午坡，昔日牡丹耀日，红药翻阶，固有是名。"

2009年，古莲花池修缮竣工后，由正门而入，迎面便为假山叠嶂，山上缀以五叶地锦，春色满坡，与园外喧嚣闹市瞬间隔绝，古莲花池内琼楼仙阁掩映其后，带有几分神秘的蓬莱之感。五叶地锦将游人引入绿色恬静之所，造景手法与南方古典园林有异曲同工之妙。由封闭静止的小空间，骤然转入开阔动态的大空间，充分体现了我国"先抑后扬"的造园艺术手法。

春午坡南面现植有牡丹数丛，虽不及园林鼎盛期的壮观景象，但散植几株也别有趣味。春末牡丹花开，花红叶绿，山石相配，石缝中间迎春点缀，呈现一派欣欣向荣之景色。春午坡两旁两棵高大魁梧的侧柏，左侧一棵用铁架支撑，树干上可见"河北城镇古树名木标志牌"，详细写有"侧柏，树龄120年，保护等级三级"。

春午坡

而今，春午坡山石仍在，坡上有当年乾隆御书碑刻。濯锦亭依旧屹立，亭旁那一道横贯东西的游廊，已改为“莲漪夏艳”牌坊，明职亭院则改为直隶图书馆。

延伸阅读：乾隆御书留碑刻

古莲花池的鼎盛时期，恰逢乾隆时期。据详细统计考证，乾隆一生中曾经七次驾临古莲花池，五次视察莲池书院。园中旧藏有许多乾隆御书碑刻，原件大部分是赐给直隶省下层官员的作品，由直隶省官员摹刻为碑。

在“莲池十二景”中，保存有乾隆御书碑刻的只有两处，一处是篇留洞，另一处便是春午坡。三通诗碑均立于春午坡南侧，如今已无法看清上面的文字。

“菲史枕经”碑

“菲史枕经正务宜，余闲亦弗碍拈诗。司空廿四品言尽，视此春晴日午时。”这首诗写于乾隆五十一年（1786）乾隆第六次驾临古莲花池之时，那时乾隆已经75岁。

“菲史枕经”的意思是把经书史籍当垫子、枕头用，形容沉迷于经史。“司空”是指唐代诗人司空图，其著有《二十四诗品》，将我国古代诗格归纳为雄浑、冲淡等二十四类。乾隆用这首诗表达自己平时沉迷于经史，正事处理适当，剩余的闲暇也不妨碍提笔作诗。司空图用二十四品把诗的风格说全了，春午坡春晴日午时分烂漫多彩的景象可以相比拟。

“直省督勤”碑

“直省督勤书院规，保阳独此号莲池。风开首善为倡率，文运方当日午时。”这首诗写于乾隆四十六年（1781）乾隆第五次驾临古莲花池之时。

“直省”即直隶省。清代直隶省除包括今河北省和北京市、天津市外，还领有与今辽宁、山东、河南、内蒙古相邻的一小部分地区。“督勤”意在表明总督勤于政事。“书院规”指的是莲池书院符合办学规范。“保阳”是保定的别称，因府治在府河北岸，有水北为阳之意。“首善”意为最好的地方，本指首都，亦泛称畿辅之地。我们可以读到，乾隆盛赞直隶省文章经籍之学的气运，正如春午坡的牡丹花处于浓艳盛开的日午时段。

“偶来停驻”碑

“偶来停驻过墙鞭，即景因思表圣篇。廿四品中无五字，研精日午恰春前。”这是81岁的乾隆最后一次为“莲池十二景”作诗，诗写于乾隆五十七年（1792）乾隆第七次驾临古莲花池之时。

“鞭”即督策，行宫界墙以西为莲池书院，故谓乾隆偶来驻跸后即过墙至莲池书院督策诸生。“圣篇”仍旧是司空图所著的《二十四诗品》。“五字”指的是苏轼《雨中看牡丹三首（其二）》诗中“午景发浓艳”之句，也就是“春午坡”名字的由来。

The Screen of Lotus Pond, Spring Noon Slope

Zhao Lin　Wang Deming

In early winter, when you enter the Ancient Lotus Pond, you may find the rockeries in front, known as the Spring Noon Slope, which look like a beautiful screen, making it one of the "Twelve Scenes of the Lotus Pond" and acclaimed as the "First Mountain in Penglai Fairyland".

In the 10th year of Qianlong's reign in the Qing Dynasty (1745), the Lotus Pond was selected as the place for the imperial palace. Since 1749, under the supervision of the local governor Fang Guancheng, the pavilions, corridors and buildings here took on a new look. Emperor Qian Long recalled the scene in his poem in 1781, "the freshness of the pavilion must attribute to Fang". In the 25th year of Qianlong (1760), Fang Guancheng grouped the scenery of the Lotus Pond into 12 parts and drew 12 pictures respectively. Although the "Twelve Scenes of the Lotus Pond" are ranked randomly, people always regard the "Spring Noon Slope" as the first scene, perhaps because it is the first thing they see when they enter the Ancient Lotus Pond. In the 26th year of Qianlong (1761), Qianlong returned from his third tour of Wutai Mountain in the West and stayed in Baoding. Fang Guancheng presented all the 12 framed pictures of the Lotus Pond to Qianlong. We can trace the descriptions of the Spring Noon Slope in Fang's words about twelve scenes.

"This slope is the screen in the entrance. A decorated pavilion appears in sight, the corridor is besides, rocks are piled together, then the slope reveals. Hundreds of peonies are planted, when spring comes, warmness and scents are surrounded. Like the famous poet Su Dongpo once wrote, 'The scene at noon seemed the most impressive, we should seize the day'. On the left side of the corridor, there is a yard, where two tablets stood with one pavilion above, and it is named 'Ming Zhi Ting'. On it, some advice given by Lv Xinwu in the Ming Dynasty were written by Minister in Xiuning, Mr. Wang Wenduan. In front of the slope, following the corridor to the right, there is a pavilion named Zhuo Jin, which reaches to the north bank of the pond."

From his article, we know that hundreds of peonies were planted under the Spring Noon Slope, which would give out a warm scent in spring. Su Dongpo, the great poet in the early Song Dynasty, wrote in his poem *Enjoying Peonies in the Rain*, that "The rain would stop tomorrow, and sunshine will glitter in the pine. Coldness blew in and I wrapped in my coat. The scene at noon seemed the most impressive. We should seize the day. It is still early till the sunset, let me cherish all this by myself." The line "The scene at noon seemed the most impressive" tells us exactly the best viewing period for peony. And the name "Spring Noon Slope" is also taken from this line.

We have learned that there were side gates around the main gate of the Ancient Lotus Pond. Entering the main gate is a small courtyard enclosed by the wall for parking chariots and sedans. Entering the second gate is the Spring Noon Slope, which stands as the gate of the garden, so Fang Guancheng describes it as a "screen in the entrance".

About its plantation, we can read more from the documents, and with the assistance of historical data, a perfect spring view picture will be outlined.

The view of the slope has a pair of mountains in the center, and the courtyard, walls and corridors create a square space, over a hundred meters long and dozens of meters wide. There is a narrow path between the mountains and the walls around, winding southeast. It is described as "a winding stone path". Not far away, there is a small rockery, fading in and out. A beautiful pavilion can be seen without obstruction in a divergent way, this is called "Ming

Zhi Ting". And inside, there is a tablet written by Minister Lv Kun in the Ming Dynasty.

To the west, there is a courtyard connecting with Wanjuan Tower. To the southwest, there is a ring corridor in the middle of Zhuo Jin Pavilion. The corridor is open, like a bird spreading its wings. Tracing the corridor and walking into the palace, we are suddenly exposed to an open space with Lotus, water, pavilion, flowers and trees, mountain and the lake. It is like living in the landscape painting.

For the expression of emotions with flowers and trees, Spring Noon Slope is indeed ingenious in terms of landscape design. There were originally two rockeries connected by an earth slope in the Spring Noon Slope, with herbaceous peonies decorating all over the place. Many literati in the Qing dynasty had composed poems for the famous scene. For example, Fang Guancheng, Governor of Zhili Province composed the following poem: "I took a walk in early morning in the breezy grove, the rock path winding towards the place of my mind. I captured spring flowers by the side of the rock under the bright sunlight. Grasping the time is important for appreciation, and one does not have to come for the sake of the fragrance". Zhang Xu, director of Lianchi Academy of Classic Learning, wrote: "How many stone-paved paths are here and where can I find the traces of clouds after entering this gate. The place is at the first peak of Penglai Fairyland at spring noon. "

During the reign of Emperor Tongzhi in the Qing Dynasty, there was no significant change in the landscape of the Slope. During the reign of Emperor Guangxu in the Qing Dynasty, the Slope was still there. In an article written by Guo Yunfeng, *Records of the Lotus Pond*, he said "The front gate faces the north, and the second gate is inside. The screen is located in the second gate and named Spring Noon Slope. When peony blossom in spring, the view is quite fabulous."

In 2009, the Lotus Pond was renovated. Walking into the place through the front gate, we can see the rockery in front. On it, Virginia creeper was planted, presenting a feeling of isolation and tranquility. The pavilion is hidden

春午坡

behind, giving a sense of fairyland. This Virginia creeper guides people into this scenic spot, and this landscaping method shares a lot with the south classical garden. From a closed small space to a large open space, it embodies the traditional Chinese landscape technique called "fall-rise pattern".

There are several clusters of peonies in the south of the Slope. Although it is not as spectacular as the garden in its heyday, it is interesting to plant a few scattered plants. When peonies bloom in late spring, the red flowers and green leaves are complemented by mountain rocks, with winter jasmines decorating the crevices, presenting a thriving picture of spring. There are two giant oriental arborvitaes on both sides of the Spring Noon Slope, with the left one supported by a steel rack. On the trunk is a sign which reads "Ancient Valuable Trees in Urban Areas of Hebei Province", along with detailed information such as "oriental arborvitae, 120 years old, level-3 protection".

Nowadays, the rocks are still piled on the slope, with the tablet written by Emperor Qianlong. Zhuo Jin Pavilion still stands there, and next to it, the corridor has been renamed as a memorial archway called "Swaying Lotus and Bright Summer", and Ming Zhi Ting has also been changed into the local library.

Extended reading: Inscriptions of the imperial script of Qianlong

The heyday of the Ancient Lotus Pond happened to be the period of Emperor Qianlong. According to detailed statistical research, Qianlong visited the Ancient Lotus Pond seven times in his life and inspected the Lotus Pond Academy five times. The garden once harbored many stone tablets with inscriptions written by Qianlong. The original copies were mostly works awarded to lower-rank officials in Zhili Province, who later engraved them on tablets.

Among the "Twelve Scenes of Lotus Pond", there are only two places where the tablets written by Qianlong are preserved, one is Pianliudong, the other is Spring Noon Slope. The three tablets are standing on the south side of the Slope, and the words on them can't be recognized now.

Tablet of "Books Obsession"

"I have always been busy with official affairs, but it won't bother me to write poems. Sikong listed all kinds of poetry styles, which are just as flourish as the blossom in the slope." This poem was written when Qianlong came to this Lotus Pond for the 6th time in 1786 when he was already 75.

The name of this tablet means people use books as cushions and pillows to show one's obsession with books. "Sikong" refers to a poet in the Tang Dynasty, named Sikong Tu, who wrote Poems in 24 Categories, classifying all poems into 24 styles, which includes vigorous or weakened. The Emperor used this poem to describe himself, obsessed with books all the time, and able to write poems in leisure while handling all management affairs. Sikong Tu listed all the poetry styles in his book, which could be compared as the prosperous scene in the slope in the spring at noon.

Tablet of "Diligent Governor"

"Governor of Zhi Province is diligent and the academy is compliant. This lotus is unique in Baoyang. It is an ideal place to hold an academy, and it is the best to enjoy the view at noon." This poem was written in the 46th year of Qianlong (1781) when the Emperor visited the Lotus Pond for the fifth time.

"Zhi Province" refers to Zhili Province, which in the Qing Dynasty included Hebei Province, Beijing, Tianjin, and a small part of areas adjacent to Liaoning, Shandong, Henan and Inner Mongolia. In the poetry, the first half indicates that the governor is diligent, and the second half means that this academy is standard and compliant. "Baoyang" is the alternate name of Baoding, and Yang means that it is located to the north of Fuhe River. "Shoushan" (the ideal place) means the best place or the capital. We can learn that Emperor Qianlong praised the academic atmosphere here, like the impressive blossom in the slope in the spring at noon.

Tablet of "Occasionally Stop"

"Occasionally stopped by to encourage the scholar, I was impressed by the scenery and recalled the lines in the Book. Though the name of the slope could be found in the poem, I have figured it out in sight." This is the last time that the 81-year-old Emperor Qianlong wrote a poem for the "Twelve scenes of the Lotus Pond". It was written when Qianlong visited the Lotus Pond for the seventh time in the 57th year of Qianlong (1792).

The first two sentences meant that Qianlong visited the Lotus Pond Academy, which is next to the east wall of the Palace, to encourage the scholars. The Book also refers to the book written by Sikong Tu. The poem refers to Su Dongpo's poem, which contains the name origin of the Spring Noon Slope.

铮铮铁骨杨继盛

蔡萌 云娟 吴战平

漫步古城街头，沿着西大街悠悠信步，虽入寒冬，但阳光洒在身上，依然能让人感觉到丝丝温暖和惬意。穿过熙熙攘攘的人群，在西关大街和皇华馆街的交会处，一处静谧古朴、庄严肃穆的院落，让人不觉放缓脚步。两尊石狮挺立门前，门外人来人往，门内幽雅寂静，一道院门隔了闹与静、古与今。这里便是明代第一谏臣杨继盛的祠堂——旌忠祠。

皇华馆的杨公祠建于明万历二十九年（1601），清代曾重修，有山门三间，门内存正殿和左右厢房各三间，正殿为硬山顶。2014年12月5日，拥有400余年历史的杨公祠修缮工程宣告竣工，一代谏臣的祠堂重焕光彩。祠堂大门由青砖灰瓦砌成，格外肃穆。“旌忠祠”牌匾悬挂于祠堂大门正上，“铁肩担道义；辣手著文章”两行杨继盛笔下的自勉联以草书写就，镌刻于大门两旁立柱之上。主殿外观以灰黑色调为主，配以棕色雕花门窗，殿门上方悬挂烫金“杨公祠”匾额。也许有的人并不熟知杨继盛，但中国共产党的创始人之一李大钊撰写的“铁肩担道义；妙手著文章”这副广为流传的名联，就是从杨继盛笔下的自勉联“铁肩担道义；辣手著文章”衍生而来。

踏入祠堂大门，一条青砖步道将庭院中分为二。道旁，夹峙着古碑数通。其中最大的一通为明代大学士、保定人孙承宗“重建敕赐旌

旌忠祠门外

杨公祠

忠祠碑”，碑额上刻有四条栩栩如生的盘龙，碑文详述了杨继盛的生平，记录了皇帝御批修建旌忠祠的历史。

杨继盛，字仲芳，号椒山，明朝著名谏臣，容城人。他为明代忠烈之臣，因弹劾权相严嵩十大罪下狱，受酷刑，被杀。他被害后12年，隆庆皇帝昭雪前代冤案，将杨继盛列为遭严嵩所害的8位直谏大臣之首，赠太常少卿，谥号“忠愍”，建旌忠祠于京师、保定等地。

打开尘封的史册，时光追溯到400多年前。明嘉靖二十九年（1550），35岁的杨继盛调升京师，任兵部车驾司员外郎。当时，蒙古鞑靼部经常侵扰明北部边境，明朝大将军仇鸾非但不予抵抗，反而与鞑靼部勾结，欲合开马市。杨继盛认为仇鸾议和示弱，丧权失节，遂上疏朝廷，谏阻开马市，弹劾仇鸾，反被诬陷进诏狱，后又贬谪狄道（今甘肃省临洮县）。杨继盛赴任狄道，看到当地土地贫瘠、百姓饥寒、教育不兴，非常痛心。他拿出自己的俸禄，卖掉坐骑和妻子的首饰，兴办东山书院。他还疏浚河道，引水灌田，开发煤山，让妻子传授百姓纺织技术。当地民众受其感化，非常尊敬和爱戴他，称其为“杨父”。据称，甘肃省临洮县至今仍保留着杨继盛广场和庙宇。

权臣严嵩曾与仇鸾争宠结怨，仇鸾死后，他极力拉拢杨继盛，奏请皇上“一岁四迁其官”，使杨继盛升迁回到北京。但严嵩万万没想到，杨继盛不攀附权势，上任刚一个月，因亲见亲闻严嵩祸国殃民的行径，便抱着必死的决心，上书《请诛贼臣疏》，历数严嵩“五奸十大罪”。杨继盛此奏被史家称为“明史上一大奏牍”。杨继盛以生命为赌注，死劾严嵩，受到“严党”穷凶极恶的打击迫害，含冤入狱。由于受酷刑被杖打一百，杨继盛双腿骨折，血肉模糊。在蝇虫滋生、肮脏阴冷的牢狱中，他的伤口恶化感染。与此同时，杨继盛还做出了一件不同寻常的事情——廷杖后的一个深夜，杨继盛安静地坐在诏狱一角，用一片破碎碗片，将自己腿上的腐肉一点一点地刮掉。碗片并不锋利，腐肉也不易割断，剧烈疼痛之时，杨继盛却没有发出一点声音，平静的表情诉说着无与伦比的勇敢与刚强……

嘉靖三十四年（1555）的秋天，北京北风凛冽，寒气逼人，杨继盛大义凛然，昂首走向刑场。临刑前，他将自书年谱交予其子，仰天长啸，诵读他那首感人肺腑的《就义诗》：“浩气还太虚，丹心照万古。生前未了事，留与后人补。天王自圣明，制度高千古。平生未报恩，留作忠魂补。”而后慷慨就义，年仅40岁。

岁月如梭。400多年后的今天，记者站在杨公祠正殿前，举目环顾，院内的几方石碑无言地诉说着历史。远望殿内杨继盛的铜像，只见他气宇轩昂，端坐堂上，一身铮铮铁骨，浩然正气，令人敬慕。历史的画卷，一幅幅、一幕幕在脑海中翻卷。杨公祠主殿内，灰地白墙配以棕黑色的木质圆柱及屋顶，庄严肃穆。殿内东侧墙壁上置有展板，介绍“明代第一谏臣”杨继盛的生平事迹。主殿正中央为杨继盛铜像，铜像高约3米，杨继盛目光凝重，威严端庄，再现了一代谏臣的忠义气质。

步入殿内，恰逢一位老者正在仔细查看玻璃展柜里的文史陈列。上前询问得知，老者姓孟，是河北农业大学的一位教授。由于家住附近，他经常会到这里走一走，感受先贤的遗迹和气息。孟老先生说：“在保定众多名胜古迹中，旌忠祠是一个非常值得参观的地方。”孟老先生告诉记者，前几天他刚去关汉卿大剧院观看了河北梆子《燕赵铁骨杨继盛》，这又促使他再次来到这里。他说：“这次来和之前来的感觉大不相同，我更深刻地体会到，杨继盛的精神不但光耀史书，更鉴照于现实和未来。作为新时代的教育工作者，我有义务，更有责任，去了解他、宣扬他。”

走出旌忠祠，日头已偏西，在夕阳的照耀下，这处隐秘在闹市里的古迹，在一派青砖灰瓦之下，有种隔世之美。

The Martyr Yang Jisheng

Cai Meng Yun Juan Wu Zhanping

Walking on the streets of the ancient city and strolling along the West Street, people can still feel warm and comfortable in the sunshine despite the cold winter. Through the bustling crowd, at the intersection of Xiguan Street and Huanghuaguan Street, there is a quiet, simple and solemn courtyard, which makes people slow down. Two stone lions stand in front of the door. People are coming and going outside. Inside the door is quiet and elegant. A courtyard door separates noise and silence, the past and the present. Here locates the ancestral hall for the notable remonstrator of the Ming Dynasty, Jing Zhong Temple (Yang Gong Temple).

The Yang Gong Temple in Huanghua Hall was built in the 29th year of Emperor Wanli of the Ming Dynasty (1601). It was rebuilt in the Qing Dynasty. There are three mountain gates, with three main halls and three left and right wing rooms respectively. The main hall has a structure of saddle roof. On December 5, 2014, with more than 400 years of history, Yang Gong Temple has been renovated and restored to its splendor. The gate of the ancestral hall is made of blue bricks and grey tiles, which is particularly solemn. The plaque of "Jing Zhong Temple" is hung on the front door of the ancestral temple. The self encouragement couplets written by Yang Jisheng are written in cursive script and engraved on the columns on both sides of the gate. The appearance

旌忠祠

of the main hall is mainly gray and black, equipped with brown carved doors and windows, and a gilded plaque "Yang Gong Temple" is hung above the hall door. Some may not know Yang Jisheng well, but one of the Founders of CPC (Communist Party of China), Li Dazhao, once wrote a well-known couplet "shoulders are burdened with morality and justice, words are created from hands", which are derived from Yang's self-driven couplet.

Stepping into the gate of the ancestral hall, you may find a blue brick footpath, which divides the courtyard into two parts. Beside the road, there are ancient steles. Among them, the largest one is engraved with "Reconstruction of Jing Zhong Temple Granted by the Imperial Court" by Sun Chengzong, a great scholar of the Ming Dynasty and a native of Baoding. Four lifelike coiled dragons are engraved on the forehead of the stele. The inscription details Yang Jisheng's life and records the history of the emperor's approval of the construction of Jing Zhong Temple.

Yang Jisheng, (the word Zhongfang, the name Jiaoshan), is a famous admonitor of the Ming Dynasty and a native of Rongcheng. He was a loyal minister of the Ming Dynasty. He was imprisoned, tortured and killed for accusing Prime Minister Yan Song of ten crimes. Twelve years after Yang was persecuted to death, Emperor Longqing justified the previous cases, and listed Yang as top of the eight persecuted remonstrators, and gave him the title as Tai Chang Shao-Qing, and the posthumous name of "Zhong Min". Also, the Jing Zhong Temple, the ancestral hall, was raised in Jingshi (the capital) and Baoding.

The historical records of the annals dates back to more than 400 years ago. In the 29th year of Emperor Jiajing of the Ming Dynasty (1550), Yang Jisheng, at the age of 35, was promoted to the capital city and took the position of Yuan Wailang in the Vehicle Division of the Military Ministry. When the Tartar invaded the northern frontier in the Ming Dynasty, General Qiu Luan was being nonresistant, instead, he colluded with the Tartar, and aimed at cooperating in the horse-trading market. Yang thought Qiu was vulnerable and disqualified, thus he submitted the suggestions on putting off the horse-trading market, and impeached Qiu. However, he was framed by Qiu and ended up in prison.

He was falsely imprisoned and then relegated to Didao (now Lintao County, Gansu Province). When Yang Jisheng went to Didao, he felt distressed to see the barren land, the poor people, and the lack of education. He took out his salary, sold his horse and his wife's jewelry, and set up Dongshan Academy. He also dredged rivers, diverted water to irrigate fields, developed coal mountains and asked his wife to teach people textile skills. Influenced by him, the local people respect and love him, calling him "Yang Fu". It is said that Yang Jisheng Square and temples are still preserved in Lintao County, Gansu Province.

The minister in power Yan Song was at odds with Qiu Luan. After Qiu died, he drew over Yang Jisheng at most and pled the emperor to promote him back to the capital. Unexpectedly, Yang refused to cling to power. After one month in office, he witnessed the wrecks and calamities by Yan, thus he embraced the will to die and submitted his complaint to the Emperor, counting

Yan's crimes one by one. It was recorded by historians as "one of the most influential complaints in the Ming Dynasty." Risking his life, Yang Jisheng impeached Yan Song. He was brutally attacked and persecuted by the "Yan party" and wrongfully imprisoned. As a result of torture, Yang Jisheng was flogged 100 times. His legs were broken, and his flesh and blood were blurred. In the fly-ridden, filthy and cold prison, his wound became festered. At the same time, Yang also did an unusual thing - one late night after being flogged, he sat quietly in a corner of the prison and scraped the rotten flesh off his leg bit by bit with a broken piece of bowl. The rotten flesh was not easy to cut as the bowl piece was not sharp. Yang Jisheng didn't make a sound when he was in severe pain. His peaceful face revealed great courage and strength.

In the autumn of the 34th year of Emperor Jiajing (1555), the north wind in Beijing was bitter and cold. With awe-inspiring righteousness, Yang Jisheng walked towards the execution yard holding his head high. Just before the execution, he gave the biography that he wrote to his son and yelled to the sky. Then he read out loud the famous *Poem before Meeting Death*: "I return my noble spirit to the universe, and my loyal heart will be remembered in history. The cause that I have not finished in this lifetime will be carried forward by my successors. The heavenly king is wise and his institutions will be carried forth in thousands of years. The gratitude that I haven't paid will be compensated by my loyal spirit." At the age of 40, he fearlessly sacrificed himself as a hero.

Time flies. Today, more than 400 years later, the reporter stood in front of the main hall of Yang Gong Temple and looked around. Several stone tablets in the courtyard silently told historical stories. In the ancestral hall, Yang's bronze statue has an imposing appearance, unbowed and respectable. History is recorded in people's minds. The picture of history rolls in my mind one by one. In the main hall of Yang Gong Temple, the gray ground and white wall are equipped with brownish black wooden pillars and roof, which reveals solemnness. There is a display board on the east wall of the hall to introduce the life story of Yang Jisheng, the "first remonstrator of the Ming Dynasty". In the center of the main hall is the bronze statue of Yang Jisheng, which is about 3 meters high. The statue has vividly represented the remonstrator's loyalty and righteousness.

Stepping into the hall, I happened to see an old man, who was carefully examining the cultural and historical display in the glass showcase. I came forward and learned that the old man, surnamed Meng, was a professor of Hebei Agricultural University. Living nearby, he often took a walk here to perceive the spirit of sages in the past. "Among the large multitude of historic sites in Baoding, the Jing zhong Temple is a place highly worth visiting." Mr. Meng told the reporter that he had just watched the Heibei Bangzi opera *The Iron Bones of Hebei: Yang Jisheng* just a few days before, which prompted him to come here. He said, "I had a very different feeling this time because I gained a deeper understanding of the fact that Yang Jisheng's spirit will not only be gloriously recorded in history but more importantly, it will shine a light into our reality and future. As an educator in the new era, I have the responsibility to understand and publicize him."

Out of the hall, it is almost the sunset time. Under the sun, this historical site hidden among the hustle and bustle of the city shines even brighter with blue bricks and gray tiles.

『舌尖』上的易县之蒸鹿尾儿

杨旭 叶子

相声贯口中的“我请你吃：蒸羊羔、蒸熊掌、蒸鹿尾儿、烧花鸭、烧雏鸡、烧子鹅、卤猪、卤鸭、酱鸡、腊肉、松花小肚儿、晾肉、香肠儿……”我们听得很多，烧花鸭、烧雏鸡等这些食物，我们吃过，其他的就算没吃过，也听说过，可就是这蒸熊掌、蒸鹿尾儿，让我们有些好奇，是真的蒸熊的手掌、鹿的尾巴吗？

其实在清朝的时候，满族人的吃食中，就有八珍的存在，这其中就包括熊掌、鹿尾儿、驼峰、象鼻等物。这几种吃食，专供王室所用，都非常难寻，不是重大聚会或者是招待外宾，基本上也不会吃到。

最初在清朝的时候，确实是吃真的鹿尾儿和熊掌。做鹿尾儿的方法极其复杂，需要将鹿尾儿过水，再将骨头剔除之后阴干，去除油脂之后再次加工阴干，蒸的时候包着菜叶，据说味道极其鲜美，入口即化。

入关建立大清后，满族人口急剧增长，鹿尾儿供应不足，皇家也取消了鹿尾儿的进贡，但王公将相又都好这一口，于是现今版的蒸鹿尾儿就出现了。

保定易县是清西陵的所在地，原来的守陵人都是满族人，吃着皇家俸禄，在吃上极度讲究，蒸鹿尾儿这一纯正的满族菜就在此

蒸鹿尾儿

蒸鹿尾儿

传承了下来，如今已经成为易县清西陵地区的特色美食。来清西陵旅游的话，一定要品尝一下，这道菜在当地的很多农家院都有。当然，如果你不怕麻烦，也可以自己在家试着做一做。

这道神秘的蒸鹿尾儿，主要原材料是猪肝和猪大肠。将猪大肠洗净、摘油，只要大肠的皮，以此作为鹿尾儿的肠衣，每头猪能用的大肠只有二尺多长的一段。用料理机粉碎猪肝的同时，加入松子、花生、芝麻、芝麻酱、骨头汤、香料、鸡蛋，将它们打匀成浆，再把打好的浆灌进猪肠，然后上锅蒸15分钟左右，出锅晾凉即可。蒸好的鹿尾儿非常软嫩，切时要特别小心，将蒸鹿尾儿切成厚度为1.5厘米左右的小片就可以上桌了。

上菜的时候有讲究，如果是八人桌，就会上九片，每人一片，盘中留一片压碟。吃的时候不能整片一口吃掉，要一点一点地吃，放进嘴里慢慢品，这样才能品味到它的鲜香。

蒸鹿尾儿的软嫩鲜香一定会让你终生难忘，曾有人评价：无论颜色还是口感，蒸鹿尾儿都特别像鹅肝，但是比鹅肝香多了。

Yi County's Steamed Deer Tail on the Tip of the Tongue

Yang Xu Ye Zi

In the Chinese cross-talk reporting the dish names, delicacies like "steamed lamb, steamed bear paws, steamed deer tails, braised spot duck, braised chicken, braised goose, marinated pork, marinated duck, chicken in brown sauce, cured meat, songhua pork stomach, deep-fried dried pork, sausages..." We've heard a lot about them, and braised spot duck and braised chicken are also our common dishes. However, other dishes like steamed bear's paw or deer's tail are intriguing. Can we really steam a bear's paw or deer's tail?

In fact, in the Qing Dynasty, there were eight treasures in the food of Manchu people, including bear paws deer tails, humps, elephant trunks and so on. These types of food are specially served for the royal family. They are very difficult to find and are rarely served except at important gatherings or for foreign guests.

Originally in the Qing Dynasty, they did eat real deer tails and bear paws. The method of making deer tails is extremely complicated. It involves soaking the deer tails in water, removing the bones and then drying them in the shade. After removing the grease, the deer tails are processed and dried in the shade again. When steaming, it is wrapped with vegetable leaves. It is said that it tastes extremely delicious and melts in the mouth.

After the establishment of the Qing Dynasty, the Manchu population increased rapidly, and the supply of deer tails was insufficient. The royal family also canceled the tribute of deer tails, but the princes and generals loved it, so the current version of steamed deer tails came into being.

Yixian County of Baoding is the location of the Western Qing Tombs. The original guards of the mausoleums were all Manchu people, who received the salary from the royal family and were extremely particular about eating. Steamed deer tails, a pure Manchu dish, was passed down here and now has become the featured food in the area of the Western Qing Tombs in Yixian County. If you visit the Western Qing Tombs, you must try this dish, which can be found in many local farmyards. Of course, if you're not afraid of trouble, you can try making this dish at home.

The main ingredients of this mysterious steamed deer tails are pork liver and intestines. First, clean the intestines and remove the fat in it, keep the remaining part as the casing of the deer tails. Only about two feet of intestines can be used for each pig. While smashing the pork liver using the blender, add pine nuts, peanuts, sesame seeds, sesame paste, bone soup, spices and eggs to it. Mix them evenly into a slurry and fill it into the intestines. Then, steam them for 15 minutes and take them out to let them cool. The steamed deer tails are very soft and tender, so extra attention must be paid when slicing them. Cut the steamed deer tails into small slices about 1.5cm thick, then you can serve it on the table.

There are also specific rules for serving the dish. If you are serving a table of 8, then prepare 9 slices, one for each and one left on the plate.

When you eat it, you can't eat the whole piece in one bite. You should eat it bit by bit, put it in your mouth and taste it slowly, so that you can enjoy its freshness.

The tender and fragrant steamed deer tail is sure to impress you for a lifetime. Someone once commented that steamed deer tails is very similar to goose liver in color and taste, but much more tasty.

飞阑桀峙高芬阁

赵琳

在古莲花池北岸，万卷楼西侧便是高芬阁。沿北岸小径游览古莲花池，径直可见高芬阁居中而立，登至二楼可俯瞰池水，宛虹亭、宛虹桥、曲步桥尽收眼底，一览无遗。

直隶总督方观承在《保定名胜图咏》中写道："在池正北。飞阑桀峙，下俯清流，幽闼内延，复道外属。每当风清月晓，翠槃擎露，红萼卷凉，襟袖之间，别饶棣爽。《晋书》云'高芬远映'，取以似之。阁东复道，达于平台，其下为'重阆之居'。池上古藤交阴，高凌复道；花时，倚阑其颠，履萦弱蔓，袂拂香璎，俨若张翠帐而观鬘舞也。"

高芬阁位于池北岸正中，峻拔挺秀，为双层、四面开窗、双坡卷棚顶式的古代亭园建筑。此阁主体面向东、西，底层中厅可穿堂而过，南侧立面直临池水，可凭栏远眺，视野极广。这里环楼阁四周苍松翠柏掩映其间，每当盛夏，荷香四溢，是临池观荷赏景的绝佳之所。因此取《晋书》中"高芬远映"的词意，命名为"高芬阁"。

"阁西翼以连楼，严奉圣祖仁皇帝御书石刻十七，紫珉绿字，烂若卿霄，榜曰'奎画楼'。楼下文柏盈阶，曰'黛柏轩'。邃闼绮疏，曲廊幽砌，列树甘蕉十余本，是曰

高芬阁

‘蕉簃’——《尔雅》疏：簃，楼阁边相连屋也。”

这里既可独立成景，也可与周边构成别具一格的景区。阁北内通双坡顶回廊方院，阁东有复道长廊可通万卷楼，阁西为坐北向南与高芬阁联成“U”形的双层建筑“奎画楼”，内藏清康熙皇帝御书石刻十七方。因楼前黛柏茁生，又有“黛柏轩”之称。黛柏是一级古树名木，有近500年的历史，故用树池围护，池内放卵石保持通透，以确保古树生长良好。莲池书院院长张叙曾有诗赞曰：“疏根开向老松颠，一带藤阴复道连。”楼西是一座宽敞的套院，因种有甘蔗而被称为“蕉簃”。

透过高芬阁北的方院、奎画楼和高芬阁间的“U”形院，奎画楼西的长院、高芬阁东复道长廊与池岸护栏构成形状多变的自然院，取得“曲院风荷”的造园艺术效果。在这里赏景，被乾隆皇帝盛赞为“池域广阔，碧波如镜”。

乾隆二十六年（1761），乾隆皇帝第四次驾临古莲花池，御览直隶总督方观承的《保定名胜图咏》，遂在每幅景图的后面各题诗一首，在《高宗御制诗集》中名为《题莲池书院十二景》。其中为“高芬阁”写道：“延楼连属贮羲文，相映罘罳瑞色氲。那更名言借司马，早应此阁号高芬。”

这里还有一段往事：乾隆十一年（1746），乾隆为祝贺莲池行宫建成，将其祖父康熙的圣迹——“龙飞”二字带到莲池行宫供奉，此二字当年曾悬挂在奎画楼上。

也难怪乾隆感慨，高楼相接，奎画楼内有圣祖仁皇帝精妙的书法作品和屏风上精美的图画，它们相互辉映，弥漫着一派祥瑞之气！哪里还要凭借《晋书》的那句名言？其实这个楼阁早就应当叫作“高芬阁”了！

乾隆四十六年（1781）、乾隆五十一年（1786），乾隆第五次、第六次驾临古莲花池，都分别为“莲池十二景”题诗，自然包括“高芬阁”。乾隆五十七年（1792），81岁的他最后一次驾临古莲花池，写下："修己立言要读书，育材股意俾高居。咨伊于是求芬者，应在实而非在虚。"

遥想200多年前的某个夏夜，方观承定是在这高芬阁上，乘着徐徐微风，陶醉在自己主持修建的"莲池十二景"之中，此情此景颇为悠然惬意。他也写下一诗："荷香熏远水，槛影俯清漪。新月坐初上，闲情理钓丝。蕉风动絺葛，凉夜未须归。"

乾隆三十三年（1768），方观承去世。132年后的庚子年（1900）闰八月，英、德、法、意四国联军入侵保定。《清苑县志》记载："（联军）驻军保定十余月之久，莲池台榭，举成灰烬矣。"联军撤出后，直隶总督袁世凯为了迎接逃往西安的慈禧太后和光绪皇帝回京途中驻跸保定，加紧重新修建古莲花池，使其为慈禧行宫御苑，但限于财力，原有建筑不能尽复旧观。

光绪三十三年（1907），杨士骧出任直隶总督，他多方筹款，又恢复了一部分建筑。此时的高芬阁，已缩而成为单间单层的"高芬轩"。其附近的奎画楼、万卷楼、花南研北草堂等俱已不存，令人无限惋惜。在张立钢、苏禄煊所写的《古莲花池行宫十二景复原及园林修治记》中曾形容道："阁屈为轩……往日辉煌不再矣！"

直至2009年，高芬阁修缮完毕，盛清风光重现人间。如今，游客可以登上高芬阁二楼，倚栏观赏莲池风韵，别有一番情趣。

The Magnificent Gao Fen Pavilion

Zhao Lin

Gaofen Pavilion stands on the north bank of the Ancient Lotus Pond and the west side of the Wanjuan Tower (a tower used to store books). When you visit the Ancient Lotus Pond along the north bank, you can see the Gaofen Pavilion standing in the middle. Climbing to the second floor of Gaofen Pavilion, you can overlook the whole pond, including the Wanhong Pavilion, Wanhong Bridge and Qubu Bridge.

Local Governor Fang Guancheng used to write in his article, *Ode to the Attractions in Baoding*, that "This pavilion is to the north of the pond. It is magnificent with clear water running underneath. Seemingly endless gates extend deep inside, while midair corridors connect to the boundless outside. Every night in cool breeze and clear moonlight, lotus leaves like jade plates hold dew, pink lotus petals close slightly in coolness, and people feel their coats and sleeves are filled with especially cool breeze. As recorded in the *Book of Jin*, 'Gao Fen Yuan Ying' (the phrase means 'lofty morals influence a far and wide area'), which we now use to symbolize lotuses. The two-storey corridor in the east of the Gaofen Pavilion reaches the platform, below which is 'Chong Lang Residence'. On the bank of the pond, shadows of ancient vines crisscross, and the height of foliage surpasses the two-storey corridor; when flowers bloom, people lean on handrails below the top end of ancient vines, of which the soft lower ends twine around their shoes and strings of flowers touch their sleeves gently, as if an emerald tent was put up for them to watch dancing flowers."

The sublime Gaofen Pavilion is located in the middle of the north bank of the pond. It is an ancient double-story pavilion with windows on each side, and a structure of double-slope round-ridge roof. The main part of the pavilion faces east and west, and it can be passed through the middle hall. The south balcony faces the pond, and you can lean on the rails and look far into the distance. Surrounded by verdant cypresses and pines, it is the best place to view the lotus and enjoy the scenery in midsummer, when lotus fragrance overflows. Therefore, it is named as "Gaofen Pavilion" from the "Gao Fen Yuan Ying" (the phrase means "lofty morals influence a far and wide area") in Book of Jin.

It can be an independent scenery, and form a unique area with the surrounding area as well. The north side of the Gaofen Pavilion leads to the quadrangle with double-slope roof and cloister. In the east side, there is a two-lane corridor leading to Wanjuan Tower. Sitting in the west of the pavilion is "Kuihua Tower". It is a two-floored building, making the shape of letter U with Gaofen Pavilion in the south, and storing 17 tablets written by Qing Emperor Kang Xi. Since many cypresses grow prosperous in its front, it is also called "Dai Bai Xuan" (the pavilion of cypress). The cypress is a first-class ancient tree, with a history of almost 500 years, and thus it is under protection, with pebbles around to keep it in cool air. The dean of Lotus Pond Academy, Zhang Xu, once wrote, "Old tree is in the center, all roots are connected." In the west, there locates a spacious yard. As Musa basjoo grows in this yard, it is named "Jiao Yi" (the yard of Musa basjoo).

Through the quadrangle in the north of Gaofen Pavilion and the U-shaped yard between Kuihua Tower and Gaofen Pavilion, the long courtyard in the west of Kuihua Tower, the double-lane corridor in the east of Gaofen Pavilion and the guardrail of the pond bank constitute a natural courtyard with varied shapes, forming the artistic effect of "Qu Yuan Feng He" (One of the ten views

莲池一景

of West Lake in Hangzhou: Since the Lotus Pond is located near the distillery, the fragrance of the wine and lotus is refreshing when the wind blows in summer). Emperor Qianlong once praised the scenery, "The pond is vast and the verdurous waves are as clear as mirrors".

In 1761, Emperor Qianlong had visited the Ancient Lotus Pond for the fourth time to appreciate the *Ode to the Attractions in Baoding*, which was written by Fang Guancheng, governor of Zhili province, and then inscribed a poem at the end of each landscape painting, which is collected and named *Inscriptions on the 12 Scenic Spots in the Lotus Pond Academy* in the *Emperor Gaozong's Royal Collection of Poems*. And it commends Gaofen Pavilion, "In the interconnected buildings, the calligraphy on the stone tablet and the paintings on the folding screen add radiance to each other. Who needed the famous quote of the *Book of Jin*? Actually, the building should have been called 'Gaofen Pavilion' a long time ago!"

There is another anecdote, in 1746, Emperor Qianlong brought his grandfather's calligraphy of "Long Fei" (the flying dragon) to celebrate the inauguration of this place, and it was hung in Kuihua Tower.

It is no wonder that Emperor Qianlong felt that in the interconnected

高芬阁

buildings, the ingenious calligraphic works by Emperor Kangxi perfectly echoed with exquisite paintings on folding screens within the Kuihua Building, creating auspicious vibes. Who needed the famous quote of the *Book of Jin*? Actually, the building should have been called "Gaofen Pavilion" a long time ago!

In the 46th (1781), and 51st (1786) year under his reign, Emperor Qianlong paid his 5th and 6th visits to the Ancient Lotus Pond, when he inscribed poems for the "12 Scenic Spots of the Lotus Pond", naturally including the "Gaofen Pavilion". For example, he wrote on his last visit in 1792, "It is really leisurely and unrestrained to enjoy landscape here, despite the pressure from the towering building of the adjacent Lotus Pond Academy."

One can easily imagine that in a summer night more than 200 years ago, Fang Guancheng must have been standing on Gaofen Pavilion, indulged in the "12 scenes of the Lotus Pond", the project that he had presided over, in the light breeze, making him quite relaxed and content. Fang Guancheng also created a poem, "The river running from afar is scented by the fragrance of lotuses, and the Gaofen Pavilion is reflected in the limpid flows. When a crescent moon is rising, I prepare to go fishing in a relaxed mood. A night breeze blows through plantain leaves and my coat, I am sober-minded on a cool night and feel it unnecessary to go to bed."

In the 33rd year of Emperor Qianlong's reign (1768), Fang Guancheng passed away. 132 years later (1990), the Allied force of Britain, Germany, France and Italy invaded Baoding in intercalary august mouth. Recorded by *Qingyuan County Annals*, during over ten months when the allied force stationed in Baoding, most of the buildings in Lotus Pond were burnt into ashes. After the withdrawal of the Allied forces, in order to welcome the Empress Dowager Cixi and Emperor Guangxu who fled to Xi'an and stayed in Baoding on their way back to Beijing, Zhili governor Yuan Shikai stepped up the reconstruction of the Ancient Lotus Pond and made it the imperial garden of Cixi palace. However, due to limited financial resources, the original buildings can not be restored to its original state.

In the 33rd year of Emperor Guangxu's reign (1907), Yang Shixiang became the local governor. He raised money to restore part of the buildings. At that time, Gaofen Pavilion has been reduced into Gaofen Xuan, a one-storey room. Kuihua Tower, Wanjuan Tower and Hua Nan Yan Bei Cao Building have all gone, which is quite unfortunate. In the *Renovation and Repair for the Lotus Pond Palace by Zhang Ligang and Su Luxuan*, it wrote, "The Pavilion has been reduced to a single room, and the past glorious days have been long gone."

Until 2009, the renovation of Gaofen Pavilion was completed, and the scenery of the Qing Dynasty in its heyday was restored. Today, tourists can go up to the second floor of Gaofen Pavilion, leaning against the handrail to enjoy the charm of the Lotus Pond.

老字号里的老味道

——探寻保定满族何记糖葫芦的技艺传承

张洁

"保定府名吃满族何记糖葫芦，卖葫芦喽，冰糖的。"这熟悉的吆喝声，刻在了许多老保定人童年的记忆里，那一串串晶莹似琉璃的糖葫芦，叫人直咽口水。记者近日走进竞秀区后屯村的满族何记糖葫芦店，探寻这一老字号的传承奥秘。

年近七十的何平安，是第七代传人，正忙着准备食材。他说："我8岁起就跟着父亲走街串巷卖糖葫芦，祖上做的糖葫芦曾作为贡品进献到皇宫，现在家里还留着进贡用的独木托盘。"

何平安说，听上一辈讲，满族人管糖葫芦叫"蜜旦旦"。进贡时，名字更有讲究，要根据食材、造型的不同，起不同的名字：葡萄做的叫"珍珠"、黄瓜做的叫"翡翠"、核桃做的叫"琥珀"……何家祖辈还根据一些脍炙人口的典故，做出有人物造型的糖葫芦，如"刘关张三结义"是用麻山药制作刘备的白脸、红山楂制作关羽的红脸、黑豆沙制作张飞的黑脸，精巧别致，堪称工艺品。

"早些年卖糖葫芦，人们都是头顶着'挎梢子'边走边叫卖。"何平安回忆。"挎梢子"为椭圆形，周边有檐儿，中间有提梁，里面摆满各色糖葫芦，甚是惹眼。

外皮晶莹剔透，山楂饱满鲜亮，从选料到

何记糖葫芦第七代传人何平安正在蘸糖葫芦

何记糖葫芦

制作，处处皆是学问。如今，满族何记糖葫芦已传至第八代，老手艺代代相传。由于糖葫芦掉地不沾沙、酥脆不黏牙，何记的名声越叫越响。

先说选料，何记的山楂只出自两个产地，一个是承德兴隆，山楂口感偏面；一个是易县紫荆关，山楂口感偏硬，两者各具特色。

制作过程中，还少不了何家祖传的技艺——抖山楂。用干净的布兜住山楂，不停地抖动，山楂跳跃其中，颜色随之变得更加鲜亮。为何抖山楂而不用水洗？何平安道出了其中奥秘：“抖伤不了表皮，抖动过程中山楂也就蹭干净了。山楂用水洗后，再经晾干，颜色就会发乌，做出来的糖葫芦就没那么鲜亮了。”接下来，就是给山楂去核。用刀一切、手指一挤，张嘴的山楂就像立着的蚌壳，再用镊子夹出核即可。何平安说，自己也知道市场上有去核的机器，虽方便快捷却损失不少果肉；用古法去核虽然费时费力，但果肉饱满口感好，所以一直坚持用古法。

熬糖是制作的关键一步，更讲究真材实料。“这是我们何家的祖传秘制配方，用优质冰糖、冰花按比例配成，不添加任何色素、防腐剂、凝固剂，做出来的糖葫芦照样像玻璃能照出人影。”何平安边说边将糖下锅，熬制过程中，还不时用勺子去除锅边析出的杂质。达到一定火候，麻利地拿起一串山楂，从锅中一蘸、用手腕一翻、往油板上一放，冷却片刻，一串诱人的糖葫芦就做好了。

咬一口嘎嘣脆，酸酸甜甜让人胃口大开。细细咂摸，还有种特别的香甜，正是那深入人心的老味道，令人眷恋。

“为什么不多开几家店？”对于记者的疑问，何平安坦言：“固守单店就是为了守住老祖宗传下来的技艺和老味道。”

现在，何家两代人一起经营着店面。前些年，何平安把技艺传给了儿子何罡和儿媳仇金红。两个年轻人在保持祖传糖葫芦样式的基础上，又创新出养生系列糖葫芦。同时针对特殊人群，推出定制服务：孕妇可预定不含山楂的纯豆沙糖葫芦；不能吃含糖食品的顾客，可以预定木糖醇系列糖葫芦；等等。

好味道，贵在坚守，重在传承。历经岁月积淀，何记的糖葫芦成了老保定人心中一种难以割舍的情怀。70岁的刘俊祥老人经常光顾何记糖葫芦，说：“这么多年吃惯了，就认这个味道。”

The Vintage Flavor from Time-honored Brands

—Explore the Skills Inherited by Brand He's Tanghulu in Manchu, Baoding

Zhang Jie

"Baoding famous Brand Manchu He's Tanghulu, Tanghulu with rock sugar." The familiar shouts (Tanghulu) have been engraved in the childhood memories of many Baoding locals since they were children. The translucent, delicious Tanghulu (sugar-coated haws) make people mouth-watering.

Reporters recently walked into Manchu He's Tanghulu shop, which is located in Houtun Village, Jingxiu District, to explore the heritage mystery of this time-honored brand .

He Ping'an, nearly 70 years old, is the seventh generation of this brand and busy preparing ingredients. "Since I was 8 years old, I have been selling Tanghulu with my father from street to street. Tanghulu made by my ancestors was once offered to the imperial palace as a tribute. Now I still keep a single wooden tray for tribute at home." he said.

He Ping'an said that according to the previous generation, Manchu people called Tanghulu "Midandan". When paying tributes to the emperor, fancy names should be particularly chosen according to the different materials and styles of the products: grape is then named "pearl", cucumber is named "jade", and walnut is named "amber"...From generation to generation, the He's also created stylish Tanghulu in shapes of prominent figures, for example, in the

等待蘸糖的糖葫芦

制作好的糖葫芦

各式各样的糖葫芦

"Be Sworn Brothers", Liu Bei, the white face, is made of yam, Guan Yu, the red face, is made of haws, and Zhang Fei, the black face, is made of black bean paste. These ingenious ideas and highly-skilled workmanship make this snack quite a work of art.

"In earlier days, people sold Tanghulu with a 'basket' on their head," He Ping' an recalled. The basket is oval, with brims around, handles in the middle, and all kinds of Tanghulu inside. That was really eye-catching.

The sugarcoat of Tanghulu is crystal, and haws are bright and full. Everything, from selecting materials to the making process, is in detail. Today, Brand He's Tanghulu has been handed down to the eighth generation, and the old craft has been handed down from generation to generation. As Brand He's Tanghulu is unique, clean and crisp, his reputation has grown further.

Speaking of the material, He's haws only come from two origins, one is Xinglong, in Chengde, which are soft, and the other is Zijingguan, in Yixian, which are hard, both are distinctive.

Shaking haws is a traditional technique passed down from generation to generation in the He family. A clean cloth is used to wrap around the haws and then constantly shake them to allow haws to dance within. The result is brighter haw colors. Why shake haws instead of washing? He Ping'an explained that "shaking does not hurt the skin and can achieve the same cleaning effect. If haws are washed, their color would darken after drying, that means the resultant sugarcoated haws look less bright. " The next step is to remove the seeds. Cutting with a knife, and squeezing with fingers, the cracked haw is like a standing clamshell, and the pit can be taken out using a tweezer. He Ping' an said, he knew that they could use a pitting machine, which was convenient, but will cause pulp loss, though the traditional method wasted time and energy, the pulp would remain intact and taste better, so they kept the traditional way.

Boiling sugar is a key step, where the authentic ingredient is the key. "This is also a secret family recipe. We use high-quality crystal sugar and ice flower as per fixed proportions. No pigments, preservatives or solidifying agent is used. The resulting sugarcoated haw can reflect people's images." While saying this, He Ping'an put sugar into a wok and stirred it with a spoon to remove the impurities distilled from it. When a certain temperature was reached, he skillfully took sticks of haws to dip in the wok, rotate it using wrist strength and put it down on the paper plate. After cooling down, a stick of appetizing sugarcoated haws are ready.

One bite instantly sends crisp, sour and sweet flavors into your mouth. Slowly savoring it, you can also detect a particular sweetness as good as the old days.

"Why not open more stores?" For the reporter's question, He Ping'an said frankly: "Sticking to a single store is to keep the skills and old taste handed down by our ancestors."

Now, the He's family runs the store for two generations. A few years ago, He Ping'an passed on his skills to his son, He Gang and his daughter-in-law, Qiu Jinhong. While the young couple are working hard to preserve various shapes of sugarcoated haws passed down from their ancestors, they have also invented the health-benefiting series. They also offer tailored services for special groups: pregnant women can book pure bean paste products without haws; customers who hate sugar can book the xylitol series.

Good flavors can only be widely appreciated with the makers' persistence and inheritance. Over years, the sugarcoated haw of the He family has become a sentimental food among Baoding locals.

Liu Junxiang, a 70-year-old man who frequents He's Tanghulu shop, said, "I've been used to eating it for so many years, and I love the taste."